POPULATION MORPHEUS

BY

S. G. BASU

THIS ONE'S FOR THE ROCKVILLE WRITERS—PASSIONATE
READERS, THOUGHTFUL CRITICS, AND GIFTED STORYTELLERS

ISBN-13: 978-0-9856467-9-0
ISBN-10: 0-9856467-9-9

POPULATION
MORPHEUS

MEMORANDUM

To: Members, the Ninety Eighth Congress, Global Government

From: Office of Colonization Capability Studies, Surrogate Project

RE: Initiation of Morpheus population research

C. 2555

It is the intent of this office to investigate the most practicable means of survival for the human race and ensure its proliferation after the Seventh Extinction (SE).

Our belief: humankind will survive the SE, possibly not on Earth.

Our mission: identifying a population hereinafter referred to as "Morpheus," of suitable subjects and implanting the chosen population in viable alternative environments.

Our principle: not all specimens of a species are created equal.

HINATA

It was all because of Artemis. One stupid fish was why I lost it. Alone in my Kubiki, light-years away *them*, I'm finally free. But why can't I forget?

I remember that day like it was yesterday. I remember waking up to the smell of fried eggs and Yonshu bacon; I remember how the air swirled with happiness. Mom was making breakfast that morning, and all was good. Then she left for work and it started to rain.

For hours the clouds poured on us and by midday, I was tired of skimming through the wavelengths. Bouncing the blue flash ball seemed like the only option I had left. I thought up a simple trick— make the ball hit the wall, let it bounce to the roof, to the other wall, and back to my hand again. It was Chiyo's naptime, but I was just too bored to care. Not even five minutes had passed when Dad offered to take me to the pet store. I had a reward outstanding for acing my math tests last term. I could've just run out with him, but no . . . I had to act nice. I had to ask Chiyo to come along with us.

No one expected me to be nice to her, least of all Dad. He knew I could be nasty when it came to Chiyo, my twin sister. Although he always cast this tired, disappointed look at me whenever I was rude with Chiyo, he never actually said anything to me. Like the time I trashed her color markers because she had written all over my walls. Or the time I hid her audio-streamers for a week, because I couldn't tolerate her off-key singing anymore. Dad never asked me why when he found her markers in the incinerator or when the streamers fell out of my vest-pack. But every time such a thing happened, he would fuss over Chiyo even more. "Chiyo is Daddy's precious little princess," he would croon. He knew just how to break my heart.

My mother, the rocket scientist, was smarter. She didn't even spare a glance. But I figured it out anyway. I didn't matter as much as my sister did. Chiyo was special; she always needed all the love *they* could give. And every day *they* gave her their all.

***

The visitors came to our school the week after the pet store fiasco. I was fiddling at the storage bubbles, shoving some reading material in and out without much purpose. My eyes were on the reflector I had fitted inside my bubble, studying the image of mean queen Allyson, my brain whirring in a frenzy to decipher the gossip she was spewing out on the other side of the corridor. They were talking about Ethan, the new exchange student from Territory 42 and I had to find out. I know . . . I was being pretty superficial, but what could I do? Ethan was seriously cute. Not that I would do anything with what I was about to scrape together from Allyson and her gang's conversation, but reading lips was fun business and, like I said, Ethan was cute.

"He's synching with the Parkers," Allyson's perfectly bowed and frosted lips informed. "Rosa has a thing, tonight at—"

"Attention, students," the loudspeakers bellowed.

The visitors marched in right after. They wore spiffy suits—all of them. They looked really sore, as if they had just been served a dose of the bitterest Qualihydrone. They didn't seem very interested in anything, but they sure read the proclamation out loud. *Very loud.*

And just like that, my recess's short-lived peace was gone.

***

It was still recess hours when Mr. Rappaport, our principal, marched us, about thirty students in all, into the sports hall and directed us to a section of benches. I was scrunched between a red-faced boy with large round eyeglasses who wrung his hands non-stop and a girl who scribbled and scrawled furiously in a blue journal even through all the commotion.

- 2 -

"What does this mean?" the boy with oversized eyeglasses whispered at me. He had the ruddiest cheeks I had ever seen. "Why did they round us up?"

I shrugged, slightly irritated. *How would I know? Who did he think I was?*

He fixed a beady, worried stare at me. "What do they want from us? Who are they anyway?"

I took a deep breath. This was getting really annoying. *Some luck I had to get a seat next to this specimen of chattering blob.*

"I think we should ask Mr. Rappaport," Chubby Cheeks suggested brightly.

What a stupid, stupid idea. Like Mr. Rappaport, our principal, would know. Rappy was surrounded by the men in suits, and he looked nervous. *Why?*

"Hey." Chubby Cheeks nudged me with his chubby arm.

The nerve! I turned, lips pursed and brows pulled together. My face burned; I must have been flushing brighter than a beetroot.

"Don't touch me, all right?" I hissed.

I was showering a long, merciless glare on Chubby Cheeks when our principal shouted. "Everyone! Attention, please!"

Rappy paused for effect.

"We have some visitors today. They are recruiters from the . . ."

"Decima." A good-looking man broke away from the huddle of suits and strutted closer to us.

"*The* Decima?" Chubby Cheeks said between gulps and grunts. "You mean . . . but . . ."

Even though I didn't react as ridiculously as the specimen of stupidity sitting next to me, I was stunned just the same. *The* Decima was part of a super-secret government program. It was a school that recruited the genetic best across the territories and trained them for the Surrogate Project. Only the *most perfect* would do, nothing less. My school, on the other hand, was genetically average — it sat right in the middle of the curves. Not that *I* was average by any standards. I could've easily gotten into the top schools, but this district had the best care for Chiyo, so obviously Mom and Dad needed to be here. Along with *them*, I was stuck in this dump of ordinariness.

"Yes, *the* Decima." The man walked over to the front row of benches. He had faded blue eyes that reminded me of Chiyo's. Mine were dark and inky, blessed by Dad's genes. Chiyo's were sort of like Mom's. Chiyo and I were twins, but the girl was nothing like me. We looked different and talked different. *They* loved us different.

"You're here to recruit?" a boy in a maroon head-wrap asked. "Recruit *us*?"

It puzzled the heck out of me too. If what I heard about the Decima was right, then these recruiters had no reason to be at our school. Why bother with a place that had little chance of offering quality products?

Someone snickered.

"Like they're so desperate to take *you*," someone commented.

"Oh no, not . . . desperate. There's no particular rush," the recruiter replied, halting a little over the words. "We are simply widening our search. You've heard the daily proclamations, I'm sure. Our time on Earth is running out fast. We have to find surrogates soon. We have to settle those new worlds quickly. You can imagine, it's a lot of work. So, we're looking for volunteers for our program. We're visiting every school, talking to advanced-level students, hoping they will join the cause."

"What's in it for us?"

"Fame, a chance to set foot where no human has ever been, a chance to challenge your very capable brains. Not too shabby, is it?"

"And never see our families again?"

What? Really? I turned to look at who was questioning Mr. Recruiter. It was Ethan—the cute boy from 42.

"Don't worry. We'll try our best to make arrangements for your family," Mr. Recruiter tried to reassure. "And think about this: you'll be doing this for them. Not just them, but for the entire human race.

We can't get everyone off this planet all at once. There's not enough resource. So, how else can we save the human race?

"One way is to do it in waves. Right now, we are getting ready to send the first wave of colonizers to the surrogate planets. These people will have a lot on their shoulders. They have to get to the Earth surrogates, colonize them, and create new worlds in the image of our Earth. If we can achieve that dream quickly enough, the chance of coming back to Earth and evacuating everyone will remain a possibility.

"Now, we need more people to turn that possibility into reality. That's why we are here. To ask you to consider for a second the difference your participation will make. To make you realize that even one of you joining us makes the future a little more viable for that last person on Earth."

It got really quiet when he paused.

"So, are you willing to take the test?" he said with a smile. "Are you brave enough to face the unknowns for the ones you love?"

I was the first to nod. Guess I was quite a fearless soldier after all. Or maybe I was just desperate to get away from my family.

***

I completed the test in fifteen, maybe twenty minutes. The challenges were pretty poppy, and the way they kept on evolving, it seemed like the testers were toying with me. It started with simple differentials and ended on a continuum problem. Nothing I hadn't done before. Mr. Recruiter-with-eyes-like-Chiyo's came to speak to me after. A smoky woman—thin as a stick, hair like fire, and eyes like frosted glass—came with him.

"You scored extremely well, Hinata," the man said, scanning my face.

I shrugged. I was always good with numbers, had started counting when I was just about a year old. *They* had tested my IQ when I was a bit older; it turned out to be a crazy large number. *Cheers for me, right? No, wrong.* There was always Chiyo. She was the special one.

"You cracked the gene sequence," the woman added, as if that was not expected. "You did it in a peculiar way too, I noticed. Not how I would have done it."

Right. I always did things different. There were a million untried ways to do things; why follow the same old, tired rules?

"Is that a bad thing?"

"Nope, it's good actually. Something I've been looking for."

Mr. Recruiter nodded at the woman. "Science Officer Katryn holds the record for fastest de-sequencing."

I shrugged. *So?*

"I hope you decide to join," Mr. Recruiter-that-was-starting-to-annoy-me-now said. "Since you're underage, we shall send the drafting papers to your home for your parents to sign. You might want to talk to them before our agents show up."

"Yup, sure." Like hell I was going to discuss all this with Mom and Dad and get lectured for hours. The agents would have to earn their pay.

"Want to take a tour of your new school?"

I shrugged again. *Why not?*

***

The facilities, an unending maze of interconnecting white corridors and rooms, were all underground. It was weird and creepy, to be honest. We, the lucky ten who passed the recruitment tests, were taken below the surface through the parking garage of an abandoned building. The Global Government had built a whole city under here. We passed a zillion checkpoints, each swarming with uniformed guards so ridiculously clad in armor from head to foot that it seemed like they would topple over if we poked them once. I didn't understand why these people needed to be so heavily armed. It was, like I said, weird.

We kept on going until we reached a wall of blue. The place sort of glowed with the color. The word MORPHEUS was stamped along its length. I had no idea what that meant, but it seemed to be a specialized section, because the guards behind this wall wore even more gear. They scanned our military vehicle and put it on a gigantic elevator that descended slowly to the bowels of the earth. My heart thudded a little louder as I realized where we were headed—the bunkers.

We had been hearing rumors about these bunkers for a while now. Ever since the southern territories had been wiped out after the Flood of 2552, the Global Government had supposedly started building subterranean housing. No one knew where they were located, but there was plenty of chatter on the OneNet. Groups had sprung up everywhere—people hunting for clues to these places, people theorizing about what exactly the plan was—but no one really knew for sure.

One thing was clear: Earth was quickly turning uninhabitable, even with the year-round breathing masks and the seasonal migrations. Land was getting scarcer by the day, and the waters were becoming so turbulent that the fleet cities were starting to disintegrate.

Thus the hidden bunkers, built to shelter and protect some of the population from the apocalypse that was coming sooner or later. The OneNet cults named these bunkers the Arks and the people who were chosen to live there were called the elites. The remaining humans, the ones on the outside, were the generics.

"Hey."

Someone was poking my elbow. I turned my audio-streamers down and looked, dreading seeing the face I was pretty sure I would see. Of course, it was Chubby Cheeks. Again.

"Yes?"

"What if they imprison us here? No one would ever know."

I didn't even feel like rolling my eyes at him. "Why would they? And Rappy knows we're here, all right?"

"But what if Mr. Rappaport is in with these guys? Maybe he gets a spot on the Ark if he supplies brains for free. You know . . . us."

Oh no. Chubby Cheeks was one of them. An Ark hunter. His big head was full of conspiracy theories. *How on earth did I always end up sitting next to him?*

"Does it matter?" I tried to sound standoffish. "Most of us will decide to join the program anyway. Either way we'll leave our families behind. If they keep us now it'll save them and us some time and useless drama."

The boy stared and kept staring. Had I said something wrong? I didn't know, but he sure looked pretty shocked.

I was hoping I had silenced Chubby Cheeks for good when another voice butted in. "You don't want to say good-bye to your folks? But why not?"

Maybe I didn't. How was that anyone's business but mine? He didn't know how I felt like I didn't belong with my *folks*. Or how *they* always fussed over my sister and barely had a minute to spare for me. He had no idea what it was like to be told that my ambitions could wait; Chiyo's happiness came first. I didn't say it out loud though, because I recognized that voice. Ethan. The boy I thought was cute.

"I didn't mean it that way." I tried to fix that awkward slip. "I meant that we're gonna leave anyway. So —"

"Still makes a difference," Ethan cut me off and continued stubbornly. "I can't just vanish like that, without my family knowing where I was gone."

Good for him that he cared so much. I shrugged and turned up the volume of my streamer, and the strains of the Flaming Scorpions filled my ears. Funny, Ethan didn't seem as cute after that.

***

I got home quite late that evening. The tour had been long. Dad rushed out when I was a few steps away from the door. He suspiciously eyed the large military vehicle as it disappeared around the rundown eastern end of our street.

"What's going on? Everything all right?"

Seriously, the man was what Rappy would call "intellectually challenged." *What a question.* Couldn't he see that I was all right?

"I'm fine."

I turned the volume of my streamer up a notch. The Flaming Scorpions were making sweet music.

"You're late," Dad kept on yammering. "What was that vehicle you got off from?"

"A friend dropped me off," I replied, talking long, fast steps across our tiny entry room and into my own miniscule refuge.

I was lucky to have a room of my own. Most kids I knew had never lived in a private house. This was the age of mass housing; multiple families shared one apartment between them. We had a whole house to ourselves, even though it was in a broken-down section of Territory 34 not too far away from the camps, only because Mom was a rocket scientist. She worked on the Surrogate Project—not directly, only as a contractor on the fringe. But still, anyone connected to the Surrogate Project was important enough to be allotted a patch of land. We, of the Surrogate Project, were the privileged. Although, such privilege didn't come cheap. The project demanded undisputed allegiance of its workers and utmost confidentiality. If the Global Government called for action, no matter what time or day, they would have to respond to the summons immediately. There could be no excuses, no delays, and no refusals.

A loud rap sounded on my door. *Ugh! Dad again.*

"What?"

"Can you help Chiyo clean the fish bowl, please?"

"Sure, Mom."

Had it been Dad, I would've refused. I had just about had it with his "you need to learn to care" routine. But Mom was asking, and I couldn't say no. She was the one who always got me the puzzle from work, right out of the *Surrogate Daily*, which had the most ridiculously difficult jigsaws, crosswords, and what-nots ever designed. The general population never got to see them, but the general population wouldn't have even known what to do with them. I did. I loved solving them. Every night, I stayed up late, sometimes into the next morning, to finish them. Those few hours were my slice of heaven. So, I mostly did what Mom asked me to do. Like right then. Even though she wanted me to do the most annoying thing ever.

Cleaning Chiyo's fish bowl. The bowl that should've been mine. It was *my* prize from the pet store--a bowl with the biggest Dragon Koi I'd ever seen. I had held it proudly, but only for a minute. Then Chiyo did what she did best—she grabbed my stuff and yelled "Mine." Kicking and screaming, she demanded my shiny new blue-green hybrid Dragon Koi that I had just named Artemis. And like always, Chiyo got what she wanted. Just like every other time, I had to behave like an adult and understand that getting a Dragon Koi was expensive—a household like ours couldn't afford two.

That was when I figured it out: I didn't belong with this family. I was not needed. Chiyo was. Nothing around here was mine. It was all Chiyo's. But Chiyo had taken enough from me. I had nothing left to give anymore. I *had* to leave.

***

The next day came too soon, and it came in sharp, like a rough, jagged knife through freshly baked bread.

The clock said 0615. Someone was calling my name over and over again. I tried to shut it out, but the pillow I pulled over my head was not thick enough. After a while, I gave in and stumbled out of bed. It was still dark outside—too early for school. I pushed the door open.

"What have you signed up for?" Mom stood in the middle of the entry room, clutching a large sheaf of papers, her voice cracking, as she demanded an answer from me. Dad was standing at the front door; next to him were two soldiers in full combat gear. It dawned on me in slow, rigid motion; they were here to escort me to the Decima. But . . . the recruiter had said there was no rush. And yet . . .

"What have you done, Hinata? You didn't even think of asking us?" Dad cried, and the guard closest to him placed a restraining arm on his shoulder.

"I t-took a test y-yesterday," I blurted. "They were recruiting volunteers at school."

It was hard to watch the tears pool in Mom's eyes. My mother looked so tired. The skin on her face was wrinkled, and I had never noticed.

"They're here to take you away," she whispered.

Dad shrieked, struggling against the guard's hold. "They can't just take her away. She's —"

Mom's face darkened at his words. *Was it fear?* She rushed over to him and linked her arm through his. "Think about it . . . at least she'll be safe."

It got quiet after that, the silence prickling my heart.

"I'll go get ready then," I muttered.

What else could I have said? What else could I have done but run away from them? I heard someone sobbing . . . Dad. I put my streamers on and started to dress.

It didn't take me long to get ready. I hugged them quickly, telling them that I would see them soon, knowing fully well that I probably wouldn't. I couldn't do what I had planned to do — tell them that they would be happy without me anyway, that they would be better off with all the time in the world for Chiyo.

I was halfway down to the waiting vehicle when I heard the wail. It was loud — ear-splitting, heart-stopping loud. The Flaming Scorpions' thunderous song on my streamers didn't stand a chance.

"Inataaa . . ."

Chiyo. Silly girl. She could never get the hang of pronouncing the "H." I turned around. Chiyo almost tumbled out of the doorway. My brain-damaged twin sister, who barely knew how to walk, hobbled out of the house and threw herself at me.

"Inataaa . . ." she howled, clutching my neck so hard that I could hardly breathe.

Standing there, holding Chiyo like she was my only chance at life, I felt afraid. Emptiness swirled round and round inside of me. What had I done? What made me think *they* didn't need me anymore? Chiyo clearly did. Maybe Dad was right, maybe somewhere along the way *I* had forgotten to care.

How long I had stood there clinging to her, I can't recall anymore. The pain that ripped my heart into shreds that morning is still quite fresh in my memory. It comes back every time I walk into my Kubiki. My first glance almost always rests on the little bowl that sits on my windowsill. A blue-green Dragon Koi swims happily in it. I call him Artemis.

XANDER

Thwack! Thwack, thwack!

I woke up to loud drumming on my door.

The drumming was obstinate as it was odd. That was *not* how I usually began a day. The wake-up call on Farm 34 sounded different.

"You have a purpose. You are the elite of this generation. You are *not* one of nature's whims. You are what nature produced when forced to do its best. You are the pinnacle of human evolution, intellect, and ambitions."

That was what I heard every morning for the last eighteen years. I glanced at the clock next to my bed — 0400 hours. That was not when I woke up every day either.

"Xander!"

Three measured strides to the door and then I paused a second. The sound of running feet, a lot of them. Odder still.

"Xander!"

I recognized Nooney's voice; he was the warden of the early morning shift. He didn't like me. He didn't like any of us. Why would he? He was a generic, after all.

I opened the door, expecting to see a scowling face. I was right. Nooney glared, his lips twisting with contempt.

"Took five danking minutes for you to wake up," he said, teeth gnashing every word with vengeance. "This is what they call the best?"

There was no point arguing with a warden. I would be angry too if I were in his place. He was a non-essential generic and had not been chosen for the new colonies. On the other hand, I was guaranteed a spot. Yet, there he was, serving the likes of us.

There was a time when the generics' hatred for us tormented me. Why would they wish we were never born? Their suffering was not our fault. The mess on this planet was not our doing. A crushing emptiness kept eating me up from inside until I grasped on a life-saving fact: the generics' anger didn't mean a thing. Whether they liked it or not, we were valued above most people on Earth. We were the cream of the crop when it came to the Surrogate Project, and that was all that mattered.

"What's going on?" I asked Nooney, trying to keep calm.

"Your rides are here," he replied, giving me a telling look. "Get ready to leave."

"Now?"

"Yes, now," he yelled, spit gathering at the corners of his mouth. "Are you slow or something? You . . ."

He didn't say it out loud, but I knew what he was about to call me. *Devil spawn.* That was what the people on Earth, the nonessential generics, as well as the chosen ones of the Population—everyone born natural that is, called us.

I found out some time ago from a newspaper clipping. It had hurt my twelve-year-old senses, but even though it felt like someone had drained half my strength away, I wanted to know why anyone would call me devil spawn. I had cornered Master Chang.

"Why do they call us that?" I had demanded, voice choking with anger, unsteady hands thrusting the clipping at him. "You told me I was special."

Master Chang had tried to avoid my eyes, but I knew he would tell me when his hesitant fingers reached for the piece of paper.

"You *are* special, Xander," he said. "But . . . you are different."

"How?"

"All of you are results of the Farms experiment, an initiative of the Global Government. You, the harvest of Phase Three, are the first successes to come out of it," Master Chang said.

I had suddenly figured the meaning of that Global Government emblem etched on my forehead inscribed with an oversized "3."

"The Farms started with the Surrogate Project," Master Chang had continued. "The GG needed to ensure that the outstanding traits of the human race survived the migration to the new colonies, so they handpicked the men and women with the strongest qualities, combined their genetic materials and harvested samples in the hatcheries. That's you."

I had struggled to take the next breath; it was as if someone had stuck a wad of cloth in my throat. It was quite something to find out that we were truly farm-produced, like poultry or cattle.

Tenacious produce that I was, I had managed to find a question. "Isn't cloning . . . against the law?"

"You're not a clone, Xander. You are simply selectively bred, specifically designed to preserve genetic diversity as well as genetic excellence. Remember, cloning humans was outlawed in 2110, but selective fertilization was not."

Of course, the GG had found a loophole in its own code.

"You are the fortunate, the first successes of the experiment," Master Chang went on to say. "Most of Phase One and Phase Two outcomes had to be neutralized because of various deformities."

So, the perfect specimens were treated like kings. In an age where a miniscule fraction of the population owned land, we were raised on a sprawling campus off the 23rd Intercoastal Highway that connected the hub of Territory 34 to the shoreline. In the eyes of natural-born humans, we were freaks. We were also eating into their share of tickets to leave a dying Earth.

***

I reached the assembly point about five minutes after Nooney had knocked on my door. The morning air was cold and smelled of chemicals from the northern factories, and the sky above was a sickly shade of orange. Ten armored vehicles, black behemoths about twelve feet tall with five tracked wheels on each side, stood near the north entrance. *Why did the GG send us these?* It was not like we were going to war.

"Hey!" A hard shove from Riley shook away the remnants of sleep from my mind. "Woke up finally, did you?" he guffawed.

Riley was one of my "tribe," my close group of friends. He was annoying, just like most people you'd known all your life become with time, when you can predict all their unappealing mannerisms better that you could your own.

"We all got in together," Riley informed. He meant the rest of my tribe — Avi, Taye and Junpei. The entire produce of Farm 34, all 201 of us boys, was divided into smaller groups, and the five of us had been together ever since we were tots. "Great, right?"

Although it might have been sudden, it was a delightful outcome. There was nothing better than having good friends around. Master Chang always said, "You have to have a good tribe to win," and that was truer than true when you were being cast off into the unknown.

"They'll take us to the bunkers now," Riley said. "Seems like we've been assigned to Seeder 5. We'll be embedded in a population called Morpheus. The Surrogate Project is finally taking off, eh?"

Indeed. These vehicles coming to transport us to the Seeder meant only one thing — the most ambitious project of the Global Government was coming closer to culmination. The Surrogate Project had started in the fifties, 2555 to be precise, right after the Flood. The Global Government had realized that time was limited and Earth's expiration date as a habitable world was swiftly approaching. They started seeking alternatives. They had created a list of most viable planets and moons that could be colonized. The GG built five spacecrafts called Seeders that would transport the finest human specimens to these planets.

The process of selecting the best of the human race was straightforward, but it disturbed the little peace there was left on Earth. The old and the diseased, the untrained and the weak, had no place in the future; only the sturdiest stood a chance. People who had the finest genetic markers were chosen first and the rest were ranked.

The better your rank, the better was your chance to be picked for the Seeders. Those who were selected made up the "Population" of chosen ones and the future of our race. And then there were us, the produce of the Farms, tailor-made would-be leaders of the Population.

"Why have they sent these fortresses on wheels to get us?" Junpei said, frowning at the armored vehicles.

"Hey, Xander," Riley nudged me, nodding toward a shadowy corner behind us. Master Chang—our caretaker on Farm 34—stood there, watching. "Ask your Chang, he might know."

I had no intention of asking Master Chang that question, but I walked over anyway to bid him farewell. I knew I would miss him. Master Chang told me all sorts of things. He told me that he was unlikely to get a spot on the Seeders because he was past the cut-off age to be an essential. He also told me that I was a good seed.

"Xander." Master Chang's face crinkled on seeing me. "It's time for you to leave. You're lucky to get assigned to Seeder 5. That ship has the best chance of all five; your destination is the closest."

"Take care of yourself, Master Chang," I blurted in a rush to break the silence that followed.

"You be good, Xander. Look out for your tribe," he said. "But most of all, respect everyone. No person is less important than another, no matter what anyone tells you. Remember that."

His voice cracked a little.

"A great leader cannot be manufactured, Xander. He has to be born with the heart of one."

Those are the last words he said to me before a troop of soldiers marched into the hall yelling orders. I rushed to find my tribe.

***

It had not been more than thirty minutes since I woke up that morning. But it already felt like the longest day ever. I had been put into a vehicle along with twenty other boys, including my tribe. I glanced at the faces around me — they were fearful, nervous, yet oddly excited. It was funny, how even after all the training, we were all so unprepared to face the uncertain future.

We, the boys of Farm 34, were trained extensively — in combat, survival, and the arts and sciences. Although most of us were bright, the GG required we passed the monthly screenings. These tests were designed for one specific purpose — keeping us strong. The evaluations grew more demanding as we aged. The last one that was held on Farm 34 stretched over one week: endurance races in foul weather, followed by three days of survival tests in the wilderness, and finally the aptitudes. By the time I completed the last puzzle, a fission engine module, I could barely keep my eyes open. I scored at a ninety-seventh percentile, a respectable number. I was sure to get a leadership spot on one of the Seeders.

"What did Chang say?" Riley whispered into my ear as our vehicle rolled out of the gates of Farm 34. "Why these fortresses?"

"I forgot to ask."

"Ugh." Riley groaned. "You're such a softie, Xander. Bet you are feeling sorry for leaving him behind."

Maybe I was feeling sorry. I didn't get why the Global Government couldn't do more to help the non-essentials. Was it a sign of weakness that I cared?

***

We had wondered why they had dispatched armored cars, but the reason became obvious when we reached the entrance of the bunkers that housed the Surrogate Project. The generics were converged along the sides of the fenced roads, protesting.

The generics rioted exceptionally well — I had to concede that. When our cars approached the entrance, they were like a giant swell of humanity; hundreds braving the merciless freeze of the morning hours, fighting the jets of gas that were being poured on them.

Coughing and choking, they waved their burning flags and hurled pieces of trash on us. They were screaming, only I could not hear their words over the thundering roar of our vehicle. I caught mere glimpses of the chaos outside. There were very few windows in the vehicle, and truth be told, I did not want to look at the pandemonium. My reluctance to watch kept bothering me. The rest of my tribe, particularly Riley, seemed to be fully enjoying the scene. Was I really turning too soft?

Our little convoy slowly made it through the curtain of gas, as pebbles and chunks of litter struck the windshields in relentless waves. We headed toward the looming gates that were painted bloody red. *The gates of hell,* I thought as they parted, lazily or maybe almost unwillingly, to let us in. I had never yearned so much to be somewhere and yet want to run away.

A voice crackled overhead, an urgency rippling beneath the feigned control.

"Speed up, Crawlers 1, 2 and 3. All personnel on alert. The fence at the Frecais Gate has been breached."

Suddenly, something collided with us. Something sizable. Then the vehicle shot forward. It went over a hump, unsteadily. A grinding sound that rose from the underside of the armored car spread through the bated-breath silence of its innards.

"Did you see that? Did you feel that crunch?" Riley's voice trembled with an odd kind of delight he always displayed when people around him suffered. Riley had a streak of "the dark," Master Chang had told me once. Maybe this was a part of that darkness. "These generics are really something. One of them just threw themselves at us. What a brainless bunch of —"

"Stay quiet," a soldier yelled from the driver's area, making Riley fall silent.

We just about made it through. The fence had indeed been breached. The generics poured in like a swarm of tireless bees, their drone maddening, and the pointless enthusiasm of getting into the bunkers shone in their crazed eyes. The cars crushed most of them, and the ones who stepped inside the gates were shot down. Nothing felt good anymore. Not even the glorifying smiles of the welcome committee when we arrived at the center marked "Morpheus."

I should have savored the moment, because the top deputies of the local GG were all there to receive us. We were the finest among the elite. The highest official called twelve of us, the five percenters, into his office—the best meeting the best, I supposed.

"I want to welcome you to your new home," the officer said after having seated us around a rectangular table. "I'm sorry you had some trouble getting in, but now you're safe. I assure you that these bunkers are impenetrable."

True, we had reached the fabled "bunkers." Constructed underneath the cities, in areas where the surface damage was too extensive to be livable anymore and reclamation was not profitable or sustainable, these bunkers were the earliest accomplishments of the Surrogate Project. The Global Government knew that every human on Earth could not be relocated in, but the finest and the most viable—the Population—had to be given the best chance of survival. So they built a haven underground for the chosen ones.

When these bunkers were built, no one knew much about them. The legions of conspiracy theorists grew quickly, ones who suspected that the Arks—the underground bunkers—existed, and the generic civilians started unearthing the clues until an entrance was discovered. There was no stopping the generics after that; they tried to break in from all directions and infiltrate the Arks in various ways. The GG had to erect barriers and install protection, but only brought more tension and riots. The average-minded generics simply failed to see the logic.

"I'm sure you realize your importance in the perpetuation of our race," the officer droned on. "You've been created to ensure that we have the best chances of preserving the finest traits of the human race if we survive this journey. The twelve of you are the top seeds, the best of the best. So, a lot will depend on—"

There was a commotion outside, an uproar that burst through the door in the form of four soldiers and a scrawny child they held by the arms.

"What's the meaning of this?" the officer speaking to us demanded, his face turning a shade of crimson.

"This girl, sir," a soldier blurted. "Found her hiding inside the peripheral gutter."

A girl? Farm 34 was a boys-only site. Other farms in other territories had female harvests, and some had mixed-gender ones, but ours was all male. That was my first time seeing a female of our species.

She was a sad specimen of a human. Her dark hair was a matted mess caked with dust and grime, her bony face covered in dirt. Tears, now dried, left a splotchy trace on her filth-covered face. She seemed about ten years old, maybe eleven. Or maybe she simply looked younger because she lacked proper nutrition. Her eyes were like meteors on that dull face—pale brown saucers blazing like a pair of searchlights. From time to time, she shivered from head to foot, as the tearless sobs surged through her reed-like frame.

"Seems like you've arrived just in time to face your first real test." The commanding officer's bubbly voice made my stomach turn a little. "Here's the story—this girl was part of the pack that broke through our fences this morning as your convoy was rolling in. Her mother was gunned down, but this unfortunate creature managed to escape. Now, what should we do with her?"

He paused for a minute, for effect most likely.

"You've been groomed to be our future leaders. You'll make a lot of decisions for the Morpheus population, and right now is your first trial. I place her fate in your capable hands. You give me a verdict and I'll make sure the decision is carried out."

As the little creature stood there, unapologetic and unflinching, I suddenly remembered something Master Chang often said: "Life does not follow plans, it simply happens." I had just hoped to see the Seeder that day, and there I was deciding the fate of another human.

"Send her back," Jin, always the quickest, said in his usual short, snappy way.

"Why?" Riley challenged. He looked pleased about something. "I say kill her. Make an example of her. Show those generics what happens when they break our rules."

"Have you lost your brain?" Jin countered. "She's not a threat anymore. Why would you want to kill her?"

Riley was not one to give up easily. "Why do you want to spend time and resources escorting that thing out? It's an underage female. She's physically inadequate to fend for herself. And you heard it, the mother is dead. Her chances of survival out there is just—"

"There must be a reason why she is still alive," I said.

Everyone turned and looked at me. The stares were penetrating, but I continued. I had to. Moments like these were meant to be seized and utilized to one's advantage. Moments like these made gods out of mere mortals. I was not about to let the spotlight pass without a fight. "She must be important in some way."

Riley scoffed, pointing a ridiculing finger at me. "Now, that one has truly lost his brain," he declared.

It didn't look like Jin found anything humorous in what Riley said. His silence gave me the urge to speak again.

"What were her chances, really? The guards had laser cannons and they must have outnumbered the hordes quite significantly. All of the generics have been killed except for this one malnourished child. Can you imagine the chances?"

I was rewarded with a sliver of silence, and then Riley guffawed.

"What is she then? A messiah of some sort?"

"I did *not* say that. All I am saying is . . . if destiny brought her this far, maybe we ought to show her some kindness."

Riley was caught by surprise. Kindness was not something that came to him that easily or at all for that matter. Scott, the first ranker of Farm 34 and a boy I did not know very well, spoke from the other end of the table.

"What do you propose, Xander?"

"I propose keeping her here with us. Alive. Think of her value for a second. We have secured a hostage, a tool that could help us keep those generics in line. We *have* to keep her alive."

"And kill her when we leave, right?" Riley was as bloodthirsty as the hounds I had read about in those stories of the past centuries.

"We should give her a spot on the Seeder. She'll be the living proof of *our* generosity."

Riley looked incredulously around the table, seeking support. "You all are going to agree to *that*?"

There was a hopeless quiet for a moment, and I thought I'd lost the battle. Then, Jin and Scott spoke, almost in chorus.

"That's a great plan."

"I like it."

To be fair with the process, I suggested a vote next, just like Master Chang had taught us. Hands went up quickly, mostly without hesitation, and mostly in my favor. That was my first win on Seeder 5. Whether or not the officer truly liked the outcome of the hearing, I have no idea. But he kept up his end of the bargain and obtained a spot for that child on the Seeder.

My gamble paid off almost instantaneously. My stand made me someone of note—not a hero to all, but people paid attention nonetheless. There were those who did not like seeing the girl alive, given the incident at the Frecais Gate had claimed quite a few lives on our side as well. But there were many who praised the compassion I had shown. This was supposed to be a new beginning for humanity after all, and my choice had made it an auspicious and praiseworthy beginning, they had said.

Admirable or not, I was made sectional squad leader for scope maintenance on the Seeder, reporting to the captain of the ship. I was proud. Riley was not very delighted to have lost to me, but he came to accept my new status. He could not, however, bear the sight of the girl.

Tanvi was her name. About a week after our Seeder had taken off, she had told me that. She had a tiny voice that matched her tiny frame. Tanvi and her unwavering loyalty to me was the downside of my win. She followed me around the ship, always keeping her distance, but lingering like a pet dog. I could feel her eyes, luminous with gratitude, cemented on my back.

Riley made fun of it all the time, sometimes calling her a mutt, sometimes a rat, and at other times even worse. There was no point fighting him on the name-calling; I did not see much use in going against one of my tribe, especially when the benefits didn't seem significant. Riley believed I was smitten by the female, but this was not the case. First of all, she was just a kid. Second, even if she were older, I would not fall head over heels in love with her, simply because she was not the kind of a girl who made you fall in love at first sight. She was not beautiful, not even pretty. But Riley, the irrational idiot that he was, kept at it. Slowly, the following around started to bother me, and after about a month I decided to speak to her.

"I just want to help," she squeaked, shuffling a few steps backward.

I raised my voice a notch and glowered at her. "By tailing me around the ship?"

Loud chuckles rose behind me. My tribe could not resist watching. The girl seemed to shrivel at the sound.

"I don't know how else."

"Hey, she could run errands for us," Riley shouted. "She follows us around all day anyway."

The girl perked up. "I could. Please?"

Something did not quite feel right, but I agreed. It seemed like a decent solution; the girl wanted to help, and my team needed the extra assistance. There were 803 scopes in our section, and our job was to run scans on all of them every week and fix minor to medium malfunctions. It was no walk in the park; the chore was tedious at best.

There was some peace after that. Riley enjoyed ordering her around, particularly making her handle the messy parts of our jobs. One day, he sent her to clean a carbon exhaust duct. Some other day she was up in the heat vents wiping the visors. Riley said she was the perfect size for those tight spots, and the girl did not seem to mind even when my tribe laughed at her soot-covered face, so I did not have an opinion on the matter one way or another.

One day I found her hiding behind the waste disposal box, away from where my crew was fixing a loose circuit board.

"What's going on?" I asked from a distance. "Aren't you supposed to assist?"

"Sorry," she said, her sobs breaking up her voice.

She couldn't say any more, but she didn't get up either, so I probed a bit more.

"Did Riley say something?" It was a ridiculous question to ask. Riley always said things to hurt her.

She shook her head. I didn't understand why the girl wouldn't say a word against Riley. It was not like her life depended on him. Yet, she never fought him, and the thought annoyed me. Didn't she realize he wasn't going to treat her with respect unless she demanded it?

"I . . . miss my mama." Her reply was unexpected. I stood there staring helplessly at the trembling human child, wondering what it could be like to miss one's mother. Maybe it was a good thing I didn't have one.

"Hey, you two love-birds," Riley yelled before I could say a word. "Are you going to give us a hand here or what?"

The girl wiped the tears from her eyes and jumped to her feet.

It was a wonder that I tolerated Riley at all. Strange that I never confronted him. Until today . . .

It's C.2602; a little more than a year since we left Earth. Our Seeder has been holding orbit around Corpernicus-50, a mid-sized red planet with lovely striations all across it. Since we have been stationary, the time seemed perfectly suited to complete external checks on the section's scopes. My squad started early today, working through the list, rushing to meet the target. I had a report to complete with the captain in the morning, so I put Riley in charge, like I always did when I was away. It was supposed to be a regular rotation.

My emergency buzzer flashed red when I was barely halfway to the captain's office. My feet could not carry me back as fast as I wanted them to; dread clouding my eyes and freezing my heart as I neared the top deck. I found my squad gathered around a heat vent, all staring into the round opening of the pipe. Taye, fully dressed in the maintenance outfit except for his headgear, was slumped on the floor. I figured it out quickly; someone was stuck in the chute. I looked around, making a mental tally of my squad. I knew who was missing — the girl.

"The girl's stuck inside," Jin said, confirming my hunch. "Seems her foot is caught in one of the side visors. We have a little over five minutes until the next exhaust cycle. There's not enough time."

"Overrides?"

"We're on the last one. Talked to Central . . . they're routing the request now, but . . ."

I knew very well what he means. Checking heat vents was tricky business; there was only a short off cycle in which the scopes had to be accessed and tested. They couldn't be switched off for too long, and the overrides only lasted a couple of cycles. Sometimes, when the check wasn't completed within the time, we sent requests to central engineering to take the vent off grid, but that process took time.

"Alert the captain. Tell him—"

"They can't shut down a heat vent," Riley interrupted. "That's too risky."

I had never felt so angry or disappointed with anyone in my life.

A ball of fire sort of burst in my head and set my veins ablaze. I knew all too well that the captain wouldn't shut down the heat vent — that could trigger instability in the section. There was little chance that the girl would make it out in time. Riley was not wrong in his statement; Riley was the embodiment of all wrongs.

"Why is *she* in there, Riley? She's not trained for this."

"She went to help Taye. His cable snapped, so she took an extra lead out."

"And you let *her*?"

"I didn't," Riley protested, nostrils flaring. "She just took off, all right?"

"Really? Took off just like that?"

"I might've suggested that she was the best choice since she's so small."

"Of course you did."

"Hey, I didn't think that a visor would crack. And I really didn't force her to go."

Jin stepped between us. "Listen. Right now we need to figure out a way to get her out of there. The timer's not counting up."

I peered up the vent. Far away inside the tubular enclosure, a little girl was clawing furiously at the bent shape of a broken visor. Further beyond her, stretched across the skylight at the end of the pipe were the vivid red bands of the planet below.

"Get me the gear," I ordered. Sure, it would be difficult getting in and barely enough time to get out. But I couldn't give up on her. It didn't matter if anyone called me a softie, not anymore. I couldn't give up on a living human. I was responsible. Not just because she was part of my squad, but because her existence here was my doing. In some weird, twisted way, our lives had entangled, and if I didn't get her out of that vent, a big part of me would die.

Someone grabbed my arm as I crawled into the chute. I turned around. Riley's fingers were clamped on my elbow, too tightly for comfort.

"What are you doing?" he hissed.

"Going to help her." Those words felt strangely soothing as they came out.

"You're going to risk your life for that—"

"She risked her life for one of us."

"It isn't the same." His voice was rising. The corners of his mouth quivered and curled. "Your life is important."

I pried his fingers off me. "You are right. It is. But hers is too."

"Xander!"

I turned away and did not look back. Panels swung open in front of me, equipment passed, and my shoulders patted.

I know I won't stop until I secure her. My eyes are glued on the figure outlined by the light of the red planet beyond.

AYLA

Camp 14 always smells of freshly spilled blood. You know the sort of smell that hits you when you open a tin can full of coins that has been buried for a while? Kind of like that. I don't know why. It's not like there are bleeding corpses lying everywhere all the time, although they do show up fairly often on the streets. But even when the streets are clear of the dead and only trash litters the ground, the air still carries the whiff. It reminds me of slaughterhouses, and of rusted knives that people brought over to Papa for sharpening when he still worked the furnace.

Bram says it's silly. He doesn't stop at calling the thought silly either, says I'm the same as well. Actually, he calls me a dreamer, which I think is just a kind way of calling someone stupid. I let it slide. I do that for Bram. No one else would dare call me anything; I'd rip their tongue out and throw it out to the dogs. But Bram, my best friend, my only friend for as long as I can remember, always gets a pass.

Bram says a lot of things, that a girl like me doesn't belong in the camps, that I don't need to feel responsible for my father, that I'm free to choose a good future without guilt. He says that because he loves me, and he keeps on saying it because he truly believes I'm Seeder material. He wants to save me from Camp 14, the official name for the slum I've called home for more than nineteen years.

Camp 14 is not just any slum; it's the largest of the five slums in Territory 34. Territory 34 is no small place either, with a two-thousand-mile radius and five billion humans; it's the most massive human collective. If you stand on the roof of a shanty at Mission Point, where I'm heading this morning of the 8th, you can see an ocean of roofs — sheets of rusted metal, wood, corrugated Plaionfut, all lie next to each other forming a fragile patchwork of ramshackle covering for billions of souls.

Underneath is worse. Narrow walkways, their sides stacked with trash and human possessions, meander through open sewers and cramped living spaces that humans share with rats, dogs, and lice. Sunlight does not always reach the streets of Camp 14, although we do have a good supply of electricity. Food is the bigger issue. We store, stash, and preserve, but a steady supply of low pollutant-count food is hard to come by. Not quite the civilization humans had dreamed of, is it?

Balik's shed is high up on Mission Point. It has quite a view, one that comes with the rank. From his rooftop you can see the slums sweeping all the way up to the shiny spires of the Hub—the city center of Territory 34. And if the day is clear, a rare incidence, you can see the ocean on the downhill side. I have only seen it two times. It felt like magic.

The entrance to Balik's inner lair lies through a maze of makeshift partitions, each branch guarded by one or more of his bodyguards. Balik, the leader of the Hell's Spawn, the biggest of the resistance groups among us generics, is often targeted by the forces of the Global Government. Balik has many names, and he keeps many sheds just like this one, spread across the many camps of Territory 34. Whenever he's in Camp 14, he has me visit. I'm his top hacker; I can bring down the OneNet within minutes if I want.

With his arms open wide, Balik strides up to me and pulls me into a suffocating embrace as soon as I walk into the innermost chamber of his hideout after completing the screenings. "Ayla, my dear comrade. Always good to see you."

I bow my head a little. Balik likes me—maybe because his skin tone is amber-hued just like mine, or maybe it's the coding skills I have been blessed with, or maybe it's because I handed him the biggest wins against the GG. The bottom line is—he favors me. But that doesn't mean I can skimp on showing him respect.

Balik can be brutal. He demands respect and unwavering

loyalty—for him, for the massive organization that is HS, for our cause. And he demands wins. That's the hard part, fighting the GG forces that are far better equipped than us, surviving their raids and assaults, and winning in the end. It doesn't happen that easily.

"My best soldier." Balik shows me a chair as he stretches on the red silk-wrapped couch in the corner. "What new plans have you got? Give me some good news."

That's what I want to share with him—my next venture—the "Smokescreen." Once Balik approves it, I have to start setting the smaller wheels in motion, and then build it up.

"You want to shut down their ventilation system?" Balik gawks when I finish, pulling off the dark glasses he always wears. His mismatched eyes, one brown and the other a pale gray, shine with excitement. "Sure you can pull this off?"

I nod. "I will start with rerouting the terminator boxes on Coogan's Hill. I'll load most of the malcode from there."

"All right. When can you begin?"

"Day after tomorrow. I've to lay my father before I start."

"Oh, yes. Go do it."

"Okay."

"And I don't need to remind you this, but don't get identified. I won't have a marked operative back among us."

"Understood."

He doesn't have to remind me of the consequences; he knows I'll never forget Dobin. I was fifteen then, and Dobin must've been eighteen. Like me, he was also a member of Net-Angels, the hacker wing of Hell's Spawn. He returned from a botched mission and Balik found out that the GG captured an imprint of Dobin—a photo on the monitor and possibly a fingerprint.

"You remember your training, soldier?" Balik asked Dobin, who shook in his worn-out boots. "You're to self-terminate if the Global Government identifies you. Do you remember?"

"It won't happen again, sir," Dobin stuttered.

"Of course it won't."

I didn't see Balik's hand reach for the club, it happened so fast. I only realized what happened when a chunk of Dobin's brain landed on my face. I can never forget its slimy wetness, or the sharp smell of blood that drenched my shirt.

The forceful shudder comes back every time I recall the scene. It shakes me, drawing Balik's attention. He chuckles loudly.

"Keep at this and you'll soon be the head of the Net-Angels in this camp, Ayla. Isaan is getting too old and slow." Balik scrunches his face while referring to the current leader of our team. "I need people like you, people with vision and audacity. We need to stop those Seeders from leaving Earth. The Global Government can't pick and choose who they want to save and leave the rest of us to die on this God-forsaken planet. They have to find a way to evacuate the entire human population. If they can't figure out a way survive together, then we shall make them die here, alongside us."

Balik knows there's no way the GG will be able to evacuate trillions of humans from Earth and rehabilitate them on another planet. There's simply not enough time or resources to do that. Perhaps, it's more reasonable to try to get some humans out of here alive than the HS's belief of "all or none." But it's not my place to doubt or question the cause. I have to agree with Balik, so my head bobs up and down vigorously on cue. "Yes."

"Oh, wait," Balik exclaims as I rise to leave. "I have some good news. I wouldn't share this with everyone just yet, but you, Ayla . . . you're special. So . . ."

Even before he unrolls the large sheet of paper on the table, I realize what it is. It's the "Tally of Heads"—a poster filled with pictures of enforcers in the GG, the ones the HS targeted for elimination. I know those faces well; Balik shows off his tally sheet when a new face is added to it or someone is crossed off.

"Yomann Kinse." Balik thrusts a stubby finger on the face of a longhaired man in the first row. Across his picture a large red "X" has been drawn fairly recently. "The Commandant of the Frecais Gate . . . eliminated. One more Sucker down. We're getting there."

I scan the poster — row after row of faces, of men and women, a few crossed off. *We are getting nowhere. Even if we do get all of these Suckers crossed off, what purpose will it serve? How will killing these people help us?* Balik is happy regardless, and I have to be happy for him.

"Balik," I venture, as he starts rolling up the sheet. My small voice trembles a little. It's not fitting, requesting things of the leader of HS. We, the soldiers, are meant to give without expectations, but I have to ask. I have no one else but the HS. "Sorry to ask, but . . . Bram —"

"That sick friend of yours, huh?"

"Yes, he's not well."

"No one is well around here, Ayla. You think you're fine, but you're not. It's just an illusion of wellness. We're all rotting inside. Dying every second."

That's not anything I haven't heard before. It's Balik's speech, practiced and often repeated. Words won't help Bram. I need to get Bram some real medicine if I can.

"He's going to die if —"

"Take him to Yoma."

Yoma isn't a doctor. She only mixes together some healing herbs, with a pinch of this and a dash of that, and calls it medicine. Yet, she's called the best healer in Camp 14.

"I did already. It's not helping."

Balik sighs and shakes his head. The orange clouds are blinding on his dark glasses.

"I'm sorry, comrade." He slides a hand over my shoulder. "You know, in the end we can only do so much. We have to learn to let go. Let the people we love, die."

"He's the only one I have left," I persist.

"Ayla, I hate to tell you this, but the sick ones really aren't worth the fight. Look at us, you and I. We have a better chance of survival than your friend, right? Who would you rather spend time on?"

First it's disbelief, and then the irony of it makes me sick inside. *What is the difference between them and us?* We, the self-righteous generics, are no different from those elites chosen to make up the Population. In the end, it will always be about picking the people who will help you survive. We are not any different from those Suckers after all.

"You and I, I guess." I can't let my disappointment show. A slip of any doubt brewing inside me, and Balik will crash my skull in.

"Yes, you got it right. When is your father's freeing?"

"In the afternoon."

Balik hangs his head and stands in silence. "May his soul rest in peace."

"Thank you."

"Are we all set with the mission tomorrow?"

"Yes, I am."

"See you then, comrade-soldier. Godspeed."

***

I find Bram waiting for me at home. He's hunkered down, loyal as ever, next to my dead father's body. Papa has been encased already, in a chunk of ice that can barely fit through the doorway. He looks at peace, happy almost. Finally, Papa is truly free.

"Thanks, Bram."

He nods. Bram is exactly my age, but he looks older in a smaller frame. He is shriveling every day, his face turning a sick shade of puke-like yellow. I keep watching him inch toward death, yet I can't do a thing about it. Just like I watched Papa die.

"The ice is too big, Bram." I suddenly think of how much it must have cost. "I didn't give you that much."

He shrugs.

"Bram, you shouldn't have. Half of this would've been enough."

"Ayla, he's your father. Show some respect."

"Stop it, Bram. You know I loved him—always will—but he's dead. And you're alive. You need the money for your medicines."

"I have enough. Besides, he was like a father to me too. I have a right, okay?"

He is correct. Bram has been part of our family since he was six, ever since his mother was killed by a mob at the ration shop. Bram never knew his father, so it was only natural that his next-door neighbors adopted him. Papa loved him and cared for him as much as he did for me, I knew that. We had a fun time together, until the furnace blew up and crippled Papa. I was thirteen then.

"Yes, of course," I say, sitting down next to him as we wait for the Freers to come and take the body away.

Bram fidgets next to me. "I'm feeling fine, Ayla. No more medicine talk, okay?"

"Bram!"

"Let's be honest. Yoma's medicines aren't any good. You know that as much as I do, right?"

There was nothing that I didn't try after Papa's accident. But money was hard to come by. Getting a meal each day to fill our bellies was difficult enough, and medicines were a luxury.

"You should think about yourself," Bram whispers.

"Not again, Bram."

"You're Seeder material, Ayla," Bram insists. "You got into the HS for the money to help your papa, but now he's gone. There's nothing holding you back anymore. Get out of here while you still can."

"I'm *not* leaving you behind," I yell. I would've glared too, but I have learned such an effort is wasted on Bram. He wouldn't even blink.

***

The fence of the control station isn't really a fence. It's a wall of junk. Rusted machinery, broken carcasses of houses, cars, and machines make a ring around the rundown building. You can't guess it's a valuable building unless you know. That's the GG's way of camouflaging their assets. But I know. It has been on my list of potential targets for a while.

The sky is dimming and I have to wait a while longer before scaling the heaps. I have limited time to get in, reorder the cables, plant the trigger code, and get back out. It all has to be done between sundown and moonrise, when the perimeter is plunged into darkness.

The "fence" is relatively easy; my sticky sneakers still have enough in them to make the trek across without disturbing the precarious balance of the pile. I wait once again on the other side until the last traces of the sunlight is gone. Then, blade in one hand and the code breaker tube in another, I take practiced steps across the browned patch between the fence and the building.

The lock on the back entrance was supposed to have been painless, given it was an old PWC combination lock, and I expected it to take five minutes for my code breaker. It falls open in two. Something feels off, but I move on regardless, ignoring the uneasy flutter in my stomach. I arm my smokers for the three monitors from the door to the junction room, place the first one at the threshold, and slip inside.

The smokers work without a hitch. The monitors, all three of them, go out one by one, providing me with a safe shadow zone. The junction room door, the third one on the right, is ajar. *Weird!* I hesitate for a moment, and then I push forward. I scan the panels as soon as I step inside, seeking the one set of connectors that I need to reroute. The job is easy for the seasoned operative like me.

I see a shadow flit across the doorway just as I start counting the cables. And right after that, the Revin gas barrier that was so safely tucked away at the corner of the room goes off with a loud pop.

"No," I whisper under my breath. Revin is the most terrible thing that can happen to an operative, the worst thing that can go wrong with an op. Revin, a slow-acting neurotoxin, can knock a full-grown human unconscious in twenty minutes, and if an antidote is not received in time, it can paralyze.

I rush to the door, but what are the chances? The gas barriers have popped there as well. Green smoke streams from the two ends of the corridor, fizzing and crackling just like Revin usually does. I hop back inside the junction room, looking for the breaker closet — the one place in there that will have seals strong enough to resist a gas. That's the only place I can wait until the Revin clears. Heart pounding like crazy, holding my breath as long as I can, I search for the telltale "ripped net" symbol of the breaker closet, spotting it when the room is nearly a third full with the gas.

Gasping to fill my air-starved lungs once I'm inside the closet, I scan my surroundings. It's a place big enough to spend a half hour, which is usually how long it takes for Revin to settle and disintegrate. The closet wall is full of breakers for electricity, various relays for the signals and a few switches. Quickly running my hand over my most critical possessions — the blade, my satchel, and the code-breaker — I rest my back against the cool walls of the breaker closet. Taking time to exhale, I start thinking. What could have caused the Revin to pop?

The door flies open, and before I can pull out my blade, a man slips inside. The first thing I notice is his uniform — a standard issue uniform for a GG high ranker, all black with silver stars on the shoulders. He looks older than me but not by much. His face is angular, his eyes pale, blue perhaps, and his dark hair is short and neatly parted on the right. His face looks familiar, but I can't quite place it.

"Good thinking getting in here," he says. His words ripple across the tiny enclosure in an unfamiliar, almost melodious drawl. He has to be from up north.

My brain whirrs at a wild, relentless pace. There's little room to move, we are literally at arm's distance. Stuck in a breaker closet with a GG official, I'm as good as dead. There are only three options, three wonderful ways to die—the GG will kill me, I will kill myself if I somehow manage to escape from this building, or Balik will terminate me.

Stop thinking like that!

It is too soon to die. I'm not going to die, not until I want to, on my own terms. I will escape this and get back home to Bram and lie to Balik. I will live no matter what.

Danking dried-out hounds of Tartarus!

Recognition flashes like lightning through my brain, making my insides wither as I remember. This man is one of the top heads wanted by the Hell's Spawns, one of the many on Balik's tally sheet. He is the NetCommandant of the Dorzi Sector, a ruthless, bloodthirsty Sucker whose name escapes me. My hand reaches for the blade under my sleeve. I have a chance to eliminate a top Sucker, a great chance.

"Please don't try that," he says so casually that I almost jump. He leans back against the far wall, all his features frozen in anticipation of danger, except for his gaze that flicks nonstop between my hands and face. His left hand cradles a small pipe, the nozzle of the apparatus pointing at me—a laser blaster. It has the power to annihilate half of my body in a second.

"Let's be civil to each other, all right? We're both looking for a way out of that Revin, so in a sense we're . . . *compatriots*." I scoff at the word, and he simply chuckles in response. "We can pretend, can't we?"

What choice do I have? I have to wait out the neurotoxin, and this breaker closet is the only refuge. My hand falls away from the hidden blade, and a deep breath of the stale air helps relax a few of my muscles.

"If *you* forget that I'm on your most-wanted list, I'll forget that you're on mine," he says.

Blood rushes in a million streams of liquid fire to every strand of hair on my head. What does he mean by *his* list?

"We've been watching you for a while," he says in that drawl that creeps into my ears and slides in a tingling wave down my spine. "I know you, Ayla, everything about you. We made it easy for you to get in here."

"You knew I was coming here?" No wonder the code scan felt quicker. "You laid this . . . trap?"

"Sort of." The Sucker smiles. Even in this terrible moment, when there is little chance of us escaping the gas outside, he *smiles*. "To get to you."

"Get to me? You mean arrest me?"

"Something like that. You didn't think we wouldn't investigate the source of Worm#14, did you? That was a brilliant piece of work. You, not even fifteen at the time, single-handedly brought down the reactors of the Eastern Sector. That was something. We have had our eyes on you since then."

Pride raises its eager head somewhere deep inside, wanting to surge through me, but I push it back down with all my might. I have reason to be proud. That was my first solo assignment, about four years ago. But I'm not going to fall for his games; this is just a ploy to getting me to confess.

"You didn't stop there either. Deluge was yours too. As was Cerberus. And I believe the worst of them—the Acheron—was your handiwork. I studied the code a few times; your signature was all over it."

His eyes scan my face, burning my skin more than any fire ever would. He stretches his legs, and I slide as far back as I can to avoid accidental contact.

"You must've heard what Acheron did?"

I don't reply. I know of course. Acheron was designed to kill the transformers, so their security perimeter would go bust and our comrades could storm the gates. We did good, blew up a part of the bunkers. Terminated some of the Suckers as well. Not much, only a few hundred. Still, that was something—the farthest we had reached until now. The next one, my Smokescreen, will be even better. No . . .

spectacular.

"You like killing people," he alleges. In that careless moment I look up into his sharp, pale-blue eyes that reminded me of the ice that encased Papa a day ago.

"No, I don't," I retort.

"Sure you do. Very proud of your Acheron, aren't you?" He stops for a second. I thank the yellow-river Gods for the pause. I feel weak—my mind drifts—to Papa, Bram, dead people . . . lots of dead people.

"Planning something even bigger next time?"

Like I'm falling for *that*. I am not about to admit that any of these were mine. My brain snaps back in place, alert. Outside, the crackle of the Revin grows louder.

"What is someone like you doing among the generic waste?"

A fire erupts in my head. I know they call us that, but the way he says it makes my skin crawl.

"You wouldn't understand, Sucker." I pour all the venom I can gather in that word, our name for the elites and short for bloodsuckers.

He doesn't even flinch. His calculating eyes keep roaming all over me.

"Your father's dead now. You have no family left." The danking Sucker knows all about me. They *have* been watching me.

"I have friends," I counter, remembering Bram's pale, drained face. He is as good as family.

"Your talent doesn't belong among them. You have good skills. You could be on a Seeder if you want to."

Those words remind me of Bram again.

"You think I'll turn?" I sneer.

"I'm hoping you will. That's the reason I'm here."

He shifts on his feet, turning slightly to find a better position in the cramped breaker closet.

"I live by my code. I'll keep fighting the GG until my last breath."

He chuckles, his eyes narrowing with amusement, lips curling into a roguish smile.

"You'll get caught. We're on to you." He leans closer, eyes glinting with a threat that I know is sincere. This man has mowed down an entire section of Camp 14, killing thousands, just to get back at a cell of Hell's Spawn. He can kill me without blinking. Yet, I'm still alive.

"I can take you into custody right now. You know why I'm not? Because I want you to consider my proposal. We respect skills like yours. You could use them to help people, not kill them. You'd have a life, a reason to live, and better company to die with. Come with me. Come join us."

A sneer gushes out of me as I shake my head. If this man thinks he can simply tempt me into switching sides, he has another thing coming.

"I had to ask. My offer stands from now until . . . the next time I find you on Global Government premises. Think about it. Don't throw your life away. There's no glory in what you're doing, no reward. With us, you can—"

"I'll *never* be with you," I say, very slowly. Softly too, letting my words weigh down the temptations I can feel stirring within me. "I don't need to think over any offers from the GG."

"All right then," he declares, before grabbing the door handle.

"What are you doing?" I scream, twisting his hand off the doorknob.

His eyes grow a tad wider. I glimpse a flicker of alarm that melts into relief.

"You don't want me to leave. Are you enjoying spending time with me?"

"What?" Honestly, I don't quite follow for a second. Then it dawns on me—the Sucker's teasing me. "I was thinking of the gas outside."

"What gas?" he asks, before yanking the door open.

Where is the Revin I'd seen? The junction room outside lies wrapped in darkness and . . . quiet. There's no pall of green, no fizzing or spurting either.

I step out with caution, grabbing my satchel tightly.

"Let's go, hurry up," the man orders from the front door. "There's no point looking at the panels, I'll have them switched around tonight."

He saw me stealing a look at the terminator boxes. I was indeed trying to memorize the switch locations. This guy is sharp.

I follow along, remembering the road out; it was the same way I came in and the monitors are still turned off. He leads me to the door I had used to sneak in and throws it open. The humidity feels like a splash of warm, salty water on my skin. Sickly moonbeams have flooded the backyard. They make me think of Bram again. How long will he live? Not long enough. Yoma's ground roots and seeds didn't help people for too long.

"You'll have ten minutes to reach the perimeter." The commandant's voice sounds a bit rushed. "I'll set the timer to reactivate security in this area right after you step off the stairs."

An idea, a shameful idea hesitantly bubbles to life in my mind. I wrestle it. I can't give in. This is war. He is the enemy. He has killed so many of us. I have fought for so long. I can't just ask him for —

"Take this." I blink to fathom what he's offering me — a nicID, passes that were given to all elites. "In case you decide to do the sensible thing, come in with that. I'll get you from there."

I shake my head vigorously, more to drive that idea away than to refuse him. "I'm not. I — "

"In that case, you'll find other uses for the ID. Keep it."

My feet suddenly feel heavy. I'm reluctant to take that step away from him. So this is what it feels like to be tempted.

"You'd probably have prison guards waiting for whoever shows up with this ID."

"You should know better than to conclude that," he replies,

flashing an arrogant grin. "I'd be much more of a hero if I brought you in right now."

He's right. But I know that already. I'm only saying that because I don't want to think I have a choice. How can I think of betraying my cause? But then, what good is a cause if it can't help save your best friend?

"I have a counter offer," I declare bravely, standing tall to meet his gaze.

"I'm listening."

"I'll come in if . . . you help my friend."

He looks surprised; his eyes narrow to slits and his lips thin. The commandant is not used to negotiating. Certainly not with a low-life generic like me.

"Your friend? What's his name?"

There's something in his voice—an edge, a bite that makes me tense. Why does he need a name?

"How does a name matter?"

His gaze scans my face over and over again.

"Bram," he says with slow deliberation. A hint of a smile courses his face as he recognizes the acknowledgement I fail to stop from showing. He knows Bram too? Is there anything he doesn't know about me? "What's your interest in him?"

"He's my best friend," I growl. "And he's sick. He needs help."

"We know. It's his heart . . . has a hole in it."

"What?"

"It needs repairing, or replacement."

"But there's no way I could—" Fear grabs me by my throat, my eyes sting. I can't even get Bram real medicine. Heck, Yoma is all we have, how on earth can I fix the hole in Bram's heart?

"We can help."

I forget to breathe. They will? For me? Suddenly I think of something else, something even better.

"You have to get him a spot on the Seeder."

"Hmm . . ."

His eagerness of moments ago has just about vanished. "Yes or no?" I demand.

"Impatient, are we?"

I don't reply. The silence burrows into my senses. He will refuse. Bram will die. Too soon. Like everything else on this planet.

"Please."

His brow arches up. Is it so surprising that I would beg?

I'm willing to go as far as it takes. "I'd make it up to you." I give it all I have.

"You would? How?"

"I'd do anything you want me to." I know I sound desperate, and I'm dying inside with embarrassment. I don't care. I only want Bram to live.

"Oh, really? Anything?" Amusement crinkles the corners of his mouth. "All right, it's a deal. Come to the Dorzi Gate on the 12th with your friend."

"How do I know you'll keep your promise?"

"I make promises only when I mean to keep them. But you're right. You don't know that. So, you'll have to take your chances."

I know I have to. One way or another. First, I have to survive Balik's questioning. If he even suspects —

"Scared?"

Heck, yes, I'm scared. Balik and the HS would beat me into a pulp and feed me to the dogs if they find out. But there's no use thinking about it. I brace myself for the run to the fences.

"You outsmarted *us* for two years and more. The HS are nothing compared."

Is he reading my mind? There have been rumors that some elites were testing precognition and mind-reading techniques. Is he one of those? He's a NetCommandant, so he is probably among the best equipped of them.

"You never know," he says.

"What?"

"Who we are. What we are capable of. Until we find ourselves with our back against the wall."

"Oh." I smile in relief. Not a mind reader after all, or he could very well have stolen all of the HS's future plans from my head. I can turn myself in for Bram, but I'll never disclose the Hell's Spawns' secrets.

"Ayla." The way he says my name, cascading like a waterfall in that strange intonation of his, makes me turn around. I had not expected him to reach out to touch my face. I couldn't even shrink back in time to avoid his thumb from landing on my cheek. "With a brain like that and a smile like this, you'll go places."

Falling back one step and then another, my eyes locked on his, I walk off the staircase. The run back to Bram's is long winding and fuzzy, but I reach it eventually. The clouds begin to light up around the edges when I knock on his door. A new day is on its way.

MATTEO

"Do or die trying. Do or die trying. Do or die trying," I chant, sprinting through the shadowy factory floor.

Visibility almost down to zero, temperature near freezing, and wind speeds up in the thirties. Mother Nature has set up the stage just right to test what we're made of. She's created an ideal night for a Prowl.

Clouds, puffed up with stinging water, grunt and growl in the orange skies. The wind is a picture-perfect companion for it. Its gusts are loud and sharp, shrieking through broken windows of the abandoned factory they use for the Prowl races. The blasts scatter pieces of glass across the wrinkled floor to slow us down.

I'm one of the hundred racers trying to get a place in the Seeders by winning the Prowl. I'm the frontrunner, until now. That is not just good, but great. I need all the head start I can get. So far, the run has been a sure thing. I've hit all the expected obstacles, and I know there should only be two more left. One of which will be *the Pit* — the path to my salvation, my doom. It will still my heart and stiffen my legs. Just as in the three Prowls before this, *it* will be the reason I'll fail.

But right now, I'm winning. My competition must be far behind, lagging by at least one level, because I haven't heard another crunch on the glass other than mine. I will myself forward, tap-dancing across the pieces of glass, making as much as I can out of my lead.

The light is weak, and my eyes powerless against the dark. My heart thrashes like a fish out of water in my chest as I rush toward where the floor ends and a flag stands fluttering like crazy in the mad winds. It's colored a fluorescent blue, the circle inscribed with a triangle with a bold "GG" at its center, the silvery-white symbol of the Global Government. The flag is there for two reasons, giving us racers a sense of direction in the dark, and indicating the end of one stage and the beginning of another. My muscles tighten as I get closer to it, partly in fear and partly expecting change.

The wind sweeps across my face in a wave of a million stinging needles as I near the GG flag, reminding me of that night three summers ago when I caught a hammerhead shark. I was nineteen. My Rizza had been so scared to let me go on that trawler, but I'd fitted in well.

Desperate to find out what lies next, I try to blink away the heavy pellets of ice-cold water that batter my eyelids. It's just the Skywalk.

Right beyond my toes, the floor ends. Far away, on the other side of a large yard full of junk, is another building just like the one I'm in. A pair of cables, each the thickness of an average man's arm, is placed a couple feet apart, tying the two buildings together, and the only means to cross the junkyard separating them. A tumble into the industrial wastes thirty feet below would kill or cripple. Not an outcome I want. Rizza always said, "Death spares no one," and I've held that to be true from long before I could even tie my shoes. But my death has to wait until I have my revenge.

Walking across the rain-soaked cables is not an option. They are slippery, and the winds are sure to knock me off balance. I know I will have to slide across the length. Only if the danking cold wind would let off a little. But it won't. I know that too. After having tried four Prowls in the last year, anyone, even a half-wit, would know that the Suckers chose the nights with the worst weather for Prowls. And it makes sense; if they were picking the sturdiest humans to fill their labor pool for the new settlements on some God-forsaken planet, wouldn't they test those drudges in the harshest of environments? I would too if I were a Sucker.

Nothing's too difficult for me until I get to the Pit. Least of all the Skywalk. If you'd been on a fishing trawler in the South Seas and stood on its slippery deck in the middle of a storm, this would be nothing to you either.

"Do or die trying," I yell before stepping forward. Straddling over the pair of cables, I pull myself along their unreliable and slick length. This is the fifth level, the farthest I've been in my four tries. My best so far has been in my first try, right after the accident. I blasted past Level #4, and then the Pit did me in.

I hear voices behind me. Craning my neck for a quick glance, I can make out two hazy figures standing near the flagpole I've just left behind—the other racers are catching up. I soldier on, a rush filling me. I have to hold on to my lead. Ten is plenty room—that's the number of people the Suckers pick from each Prowl. They have been holding these races every month for the last five years across all the GG territories. In Territory 34 alone, there are three Prowls every month; this one in Camp 14, and two others. I tried to calculate once how many people the Suckers picked from 34—it must've been more than a thousand people by now—but I could be wrong; my brain has not been the most reliable thing since Rizza has been gone.

"Do or die trying!"

I have to go on. *Faster!* Ignoring the numbing cold that is starting to creep into my bones, I push myself forward. I have to do this! I can finish this Prowl! I just have to remember how strong I am, that I was always the toughest on the stead. Rizza used to say that the Gods gave me more strength than what was allowed per person. She knew everything. Rizza, my sister ten years older, was quite something in every way.

My Rizza was the life of the sea-stead we grew up on. Our stead, called the Southshore-34, was a medium-sized settlement. It was built right after the Flood to house the workers of Worthington-Southshore—the deep mining Megatron off the coast of Territory 34. Half a century later it still is a jaw-dropping sight—made of 102 platforms, each of which stands on a pair of reinforced concrete columns that secure it to the seabed. The platforms, resting next to each other, form a long rectangular patch of make-believe land on the high seas. Our houses, three- to five-storied dull structures, were erected in rows along the edges of Southshore-34. In between were the utility buildings, open areas, even parks. I never saw the parks being parks. By the time I was old enough, they were mostly run-down nooks with overgrown plants and weeds. Southshore-34 was close to abandoned by then.

Everything on it was held together by prayers and some luck, Rizza said. The Megatron output was low, so Worthington Industries had very little interest left in the Southshore mines anymore. People on the sea-stead refused to give up however. Life on the stead was better compared to the slums on the shore, they figured. So, even when the work became hard to find and food supplies from Worthington Industries became irregular and shoddy, people stayed on.

Not our mother. She left when I was two—took off with a repair engineer who was visiting the mines. Dad stayed around, and Letty, the radio-keeper's widow, soon became his new wife. It was not like Letty hated us, but with the short supply of food and with her own children on the way, she sure didn't pamper us much.

Rizza worked all day and for a better half of the night helping with the house, looking after me and Letty's babies, cooking, cleaning, scrubbing. My Rizza was the keeper of us all. How she found time to have a minute to tend to herself, I don't know. Maybe she didn't. But she still managed to look beautiful. Rizza was famous for her beauty, her biting wit, and most importantly, for the awesome fish pies she made. Boys scuttled about around her, but she'd always turn them down.

"Gotta think of settling down, Rizza," Dad would tell her.

"I'll wait until Matteo's grown up a little more, Dad," she would say before hurriedly kissing his forehead and disappearing into the house. Dad would sigh, but he knew very well that Rizza was the best chance I had. His own health was never any good. The cough he had picked up during the fishing trip the prior year had only gotten worse. Whatever little work he did around the stead and in the Megatron pit didn't amount to much money. Letty worked in the fish canning shop, but she was not rolling in money either. Letty's own children were young too, so until I was grown enough to fend for myself, I needed someone like Rizza. I was not street-smart like the rest of the kids my age either—a fact that didn't help Rizza any.

A blinding flash of light tears through the curtain of clouds. It illuminates the world around me, reminding me of where I am—in the middle of a Prowl. I've made it across the cables to the final level-- #6. I slither off, pulling myself to the doorframe and crawling into the shade of the broken housing on the other side. A flight of stairs made of metal gratings runs down the side to the lower level. A dark round shape dominates the middle of the floor below. Above it, a flag of the Global Government hovers like a ghost.

"Do or die trying." My words come out in a whisper.

Even though I had known it was coming, even though I've seen it three times before, my heart just about stops beating for a second. I try to breathe, drawing in as much air as I can. My legs don't want to move; I want to curl down by the stairs and sleep. The thunder crackling outside feels distant. *Can't give up!* I tread carefully, so the worn bottoms of my shoes won't slip on the steps. At the center of the darkened floor is another flag, suspended above a dark crater sinking into the depths below.

There it is! The one thing that has stopped me from finishing every other Prowl. *The Pit.* A well with water at end of its dark insides.

I know what I need to do. I have to dive into the waters below to find and swim into the tunnel that leads out of it, which will take me to the end of the race.

In my dreams I have completed the Prowl three times already, but this is reality. The musky smell of standing water makes me shudder. I step away from the edge. Memories rush back at me with intensity that I can barely handle, my heart buckling with pain as I remember.

***

The day had been brighter than any other in the week before. The summer months were getting close. It was morning and I needed to get ready for my trip down to the Megatron pits. Almost a year had passed since I'd gotten this job; Al found it for me. My overseer, who used to be Al's overseer before he moved from the pits to the fish-canning shop, liked me. He said I was dependable and always sent me out on tasks that no one else could complete.

"You're the best I got, Matt," he said before handing me the longest or deepest runs into the mining pits. "Can I trust you with this?"

I always felt proud nodding in response. That day I had no such run though; I was heading down to mid-sec—the observation spot halfway down to the seabed—to look at the fishes. I liked fishes. Sifting through my heap of clothes, I pulled out a light wrapper-coat. That was when my Rizza came in.

"Matteo," she cooed. Her voice was sweet and melty. My heart felt light, like I had just taken a dip into the seas of summer. Rizza looked as pretty as a night when the clouds parted to let a full moon peek at the seas. Her hair was pulled away from her face and gathered into a zillion wavy braids, her cheeks lit up like the night clouds, and her eyes shimmered.

"Rizza." I threw my arms around her neck.

"Oh, look at you, all dressed up and handsome," she teased. "Where are you off to?"

"To the mid-sec to watch fishes."

Rizza crossed her arms and cocked her head at me. "Why? No work today?"

"Downtime," I said proudly, feeling important that I used a word I'd heard Dad say.

Rizza raised one eyebrow at me. "Oh!"

I laughed, feeling warm in my face.

"You like this job, Matteo?"

I nodded as vigorously as I could. Of course I liked it. I *loved* it.

"They're not harassing you or anything?"

"No."

"If they do, you need to tell me. I'll tell Al, okay?"

Al was Rizza's newly wedded husband, the one who'd gotten me this spot in the Megatron crew.

I nodded again.

"I can't stop worrying about you, Matt." Rizza placed a hand on my shoulder. "You're like my baby."

"No, I'm your baby brother. You're going to have your own baby soon."

Rizza laughed, the sound filling the room to its brim. My heart puffed up again. My Rizza was going to have a baby and I would be an uncle. I'd already picked a name for him or her — Pip.

"Hey, can I come with you to mid-sec?"

"You would?" I shrieked. We could watch fishes, just like old times when Rizza and I went down to mid-sec with Dad. "Don't you have work?"

"Downtime," she replied, winking.

***

I should've left when the feeder pipes rumbled. They never rumbled; they were the quietest part of the uptake tubes. I should've realized something was wrong. But I didn't. Not until the tremor spread upward through the shaft and knocked the chairs over. Then I pulled Rizza to her feet and dashed to the elevators. They were jammed. The heat rose, and I heard that terrible noise, like the spine of a monster had cracked. "To the stairs," I shouted, pulling Rizza along. People rushed around us. We ran. The fire came from the bottom of the stairwell, the water burst in from all sides. The water and the fire were the best of friends, playing with us, chasing us up and down the stairs, long tendrils of fire nipping at our faces, the flood tearing away pieces of the metal shell that rose around us. We got to the safe floor somehow, Rizza and I and three others, but we could go no more. The walls of the stairwell gave way, and an angry spout of water burst in with a roar. It crashed on us, first plucked away the reedy man at the end of our line, and then it swept over the rest of us. With one hand grabbing the beat-up railing and the other holding Rizza, I kept moving. We had to reach the top before the stairwell filled up with water, and it was filling up pretty fast. Another chunk of the wall broke away, and a monstrous wave crashed in, throwing me back against the wall with its might. Even before I caught my breath, I realized Rizza's hand was not in mine. "Rizzaaa!" I couldn't see her anywhere. My guts crumbled and turned into a senseless mush and I couldn't breathe anymore. I wanted to die. I wanted to go find her, but I didn't know where. I tried swimming downward, but the surging water wouldn't let me. I let it carry me away instead — through the dark, water-filled stairwell, all the way up until I broke the surface. The Gods had built me well. I lived.

***

A week after I lost Rizza, my friend Robin and I were sitting side by side at the palm clump, gazing at the seas.

"Matt, you have to get out this daze," Robin said. "You have to get back to the stead. That's where you belong."

Thinking of the stead made me tremble. The water . . .

"You have to face it, Matt. Like it or not, you lived. Now you have to keep on living." He paused, looked carefully at me, and added, "She would've wanted you to."

I knew that. I also knew what had happened was wrong. Rizza had no business dying; she didn't deserve this.

"They didn't even find out how the Megatron broke."

"You have to stop thinking about *them*. Worthington Industries doesn't care. They never did, and they just don't give a dank. They have their money and they're going away with it."

"Going where?"

Robin sighed noisily. "Come on, Matteo. Think. To the new colonies, of course. They're all going on the Seeders. The whole clan of Worthingtons."

"But my Rizza is dead." A wail tore through my throat, pushing past that sticky lump of pain. "Someone was supposed to have replaced those feeder pipes on time, but didn't. They knew the pipes were jamming, but they didn't send us replacements. That's why my sister is dead. Someone should pay for not fixing those danking pipes."

"Yeah, but—"

"If they won't come, I'll find them."

"Like how? By magic?"

"I'll find where they live and—"

"Come on, Matteo." Robin slipped an arm across my slumped shoulders. "They're in the bunkers already. Hidden away. Prepping for the journey. You can't reach them."

People like the Worthingtons were always like that. Hidden away. Far from the folks who made them who they were. Just like those leaves of the palms, dancing in the breeze and reaching for the orange clouds, far off from the roots down below, clutching the leeched ground to keep them alive.

"Unless . . ."

"Unless what?" My brain snapped out of the haze of pain and focused on Robin's thoughtful face. Robin was smart, and he had thought of something. "Robin?"

"The Prowls," he said, flashing a worried yet hopeful look at me, the kind of look you get when you've discovered something new that scares you and excites you at the same time. "You've always been the strongest on the stead and . . ."

The forever-present clouds in the sky parted at his words, revealing the bluest skies above—at least, it had felt like such. He was right; my legs always carried me the quickest across the stead.

"I could," I said, feeling giddy inside like I hadn't felt in a while. "I could, I could. I could get in that way. When's the next Prowl?"

"Next month. But even if you do get in, you'd have to find them, and what would you do exactly?"

"I'll make them pay," I declared, fists curling as I rose to my feet. I had to train, hard. I had to get in.

"What does that even mean?" Robin yelled from behind, rushing to keep up with me.

"I'll show them how it feels to lose one of their own. When's the next Prowl?"

***

Someone bumps into me, almost knocking me down into the dark mouth of the Pit. I somehow manage to keep my footing. It's the girl from Camp 20. She dives like a gull into the darkness, the sound of a splash reaches my fearful ears moments later. That girl will make it to the Seeder. Another splash, and another. The Pit swallows them up one by one and stares at me. Snickers too. I'm so close, yet so far away. Three of the racers are already ahead of me.

"Do or die trying," I mutter.

It's now or never. This is to be the last Prowl, that's what the Sucker-in-charge said before the race started. What was his name again? Commandant Hung? One big-headed Sucker that one was— kept making fun of my fear of the water. Last chance to try to stop being a coward, he said, taunting me. I could've died of shame. I didn't. I stood there instead, looking at the grimy floor, realizing that stuck-up or not, the guy was right—this was my last chance to get in, to make them pay for my Rizza's death.

And now, I'm letting that chance slip away.

"Do or die trying," I shout, hoping the words will drive all fears away.

Shutting my eyes, I try to remember Rizza—her dark hair

blowing in the wind, eyes laughing even when her mouth did not, and the freckles on her face dark under the glare of the sun. I open my eyes when I hear another splash. That's four runners ahead of me. Rizza taught me to count. She was so happy when I finally made it to a hundred, telling everyone on the stead that her little brother could go all the way to three digits. I have to make her proud again, wherever she is. *I have to.*

More sounds, more footsteps. *Can't let my last chance pass by.*

Whispering Rizza's name, I step off the rim. Tumbling through the dark, I ready myself to tear through the unseen waters ahead.

DEE DEE

Today's been what Gramps would've called a seminal day. It brought me a lot of firsts: my first induction ceremony at the Decima on Seeder 5, my first holding in a quarantine tube, my first shot of Qualihydrone, and my first time meeting Reese.

Right from the start, things felt a little whicky. One minute I was dressed in my bright and shiny, red-and-gold induction robes, sitting next to my bunkmate, Pompy, in the ceremony hall, all nervous and excited. The next I was staring at a boy in the aisle across from me like I had never seen a boy before. To my defense, his family stood out like a purple apple in a basketful of oranges. That he had any family at all with him at Decima's induction ceremony was odd.

Not that I'm an orphan on this ship, but my folks are not housed in the same level as I. They got berths on this craft because of me, but their rooms are in one of the lower levels. We, the students of Decima, live in the safest, grandest section of the Seeder — the mid-deck. We meet with our families once, maybe two times every month, but that's it. They were not even invited to the induction.

The boy I was staring at, on the other hand, was surrounded by his clan. What a large clan it was too — parents and four brothers, all older than the brown-haired wiry kid in red-and-gold induction ceremony robes who sat so absolutely still that you *had* to notice. Was something odd about that stillness, as if he were dead. But then I noticed his fingers, drumming each other nonstop, all through the introductory speeches. I couldn't stop staring.

Principal Master Sapoor announced the dignitaries and I figured right away why the boy's family was there with him. It was because his father was the second-in-command of this Seeder. Imagine that.

No wonder the whole clan was allowed at the son's induction.

"Must be one spoiled brat," Pompy inferred as the sec-commander was invited to pin the Decima badges on the new inductees. "Wonder which hall he will land in. Hope not in ours."

My bleeper lit up and then Pompy's. It was time to line up. Across from us, the boy rose as well. Was funny that he ended up placed between Pompy and I. Pompy went first to get her badge from sec-comm. As soon as she was back behind the curtains proudly wearing the badge on her lapel, the principal master called the boy's name.

"Reese Michael Jarvis Worthington the Fifth, our next inductee, also the top scorer of the entrance level." Principal Master Sapoor, announcer of the event, beamed.

Holy apples of Rumba! What a name! Sounded like from a bazillion years ago when people had names like that, when names told stories of origins, of nations, of ancestry. Nations are no more. Origins hardly matter. The only thing humans care to remember now is they have sprung from monkeys. We barely even use last names anymore, except on special occasions. On the Seeder, our nicID, short for unique identifier, is a long jumble of numbers, letters, and symbols. That's how we are all tracked. In a few more years we might forget last names even existed. But not Reese. He held on to all his names. Was a pureblood from the West, for sure.

Pompy made a face. "Scion of the privileged class," she declared with a hopeless shake of her head.

Pompy likes using words that makes everyone turn around and take notice. She also likes to talk about the "classes" a lot. Reminds me of Gramps. He didn't get a seat on the Seeder — too old to be useful, they said. So unfair! No one could fly a kite like Gramps did, or repair the wheels of our racers for that matter. He was plenty useful.

"Dee Dee Nahoum, please come to the stage."

Must have phased out for a bit. Pompy nudged me. "Go on."

I stumbled forward just as Reese was entering the curtained side, bumping into him quite forcefully. His hand was strong as it grabbed mine, steadying me. His eyes, still odd and fixed, looked into mine.

"All right?"

"Yes."

"Dee Dee." The principal master was getting impatient on stage.

Reese let go and I strode forward. The sec-commander had just about finished pinning my badge when Sapoor howled, "Sir, move back, please."

I was stunned and so was the commander. Both of us stood there, puzzled and frozen in our spots, while Sapoor started yelling on his wrist-com.

"Need a quarantine crew. Now!"

He looked fearfully at my arm—tendril-like patterns had sprouted from the tip of my fingers, sprawling upward and disappearing under the sleeves of my robe. My throat dried up at the sight. How, by the apples of Rumba, did that happen?

Would've gladly broken a leg or an arm to not have what the pattern meant I had—the king of viruses, the Roban-Qu—the worst disease humankind has come across yet. Deadly, as in if not treated promptly, the blood vessels rupture and make the body a pile of mush from inside. Thankfully, it's not contagious until the final stages, but that didn't stop people from panicking at the sight of the symptoms, like Sapoor did. Roban-Qu is curable too, but only with a prolonged treatment with Qualihydrone, which is almost as much of a pain as the virus. But I couldn't figure how I could have contracted Roban-Qu on the Seeder. The only thing I could think of was that boy. Reese had grabbed my arm.

I tried to find him. Craned my neck to look behind the curtains. Only Pompy stood there, her eyes flitting over us, her face tight with worry. I looked for Reese in the audience, but he was not there either. The boy had simply vanished.

I've been stuck inside a quarantine tube since then. Have had my first shot of Qualihydrone as well. I will say this—not my favorite day. At least they gave me some books and a few pages to write on.

December 20, 2602: 1500 hours

The doctors just left. They had come by with my screenings. Guess what? They found I'm "clean." This is no Roban-Qu after all. The tendrils have started to fade away also. It's all quite mysterious. The doctors don't want to take any chances, so I'm to be kept inside the tube for two days and also kept on the Qualihydrone shots. They said I can have visitors.

December 20, 2602: 1800 hours

The info-massers are such a pain. Kept on asking questions. What did I eat over the last week? Where was I? Who was I with? Had there been any changes in my daily routine in the recent past?

I could tell that my answers disappointed them. There had been no intriguing changes in my life, no strange phenomenon I could share with them. I was eating and drinking and breathing the same way as I have been since I got on this Seeder a year or so ago. Only new thing was that boy — Reese. But, he just touched my arm for a second, that couldn't mean anything. I have to try to forget about him.

December 20, 2602: 1830 hours

Pompy showed up right after the info-massers left. I was too tired, but she got me some more books. Also, she did most of the talking, like usual.

"The induction ceremony was stalled because of *you*," she accused. "And I was in *really* big trouble. I was about to get a Qualihydrone shot because I'm your bunkmate."

"Sorry, I—"

"What did they do to you?" she demanded promptly.

Told her everything.

"Told you that boy was bad news."

"How can you be sure?"

"I just know, all right? You should've told them about him." She glared at me through the double panes of the isolation tube. "Tell them before it's too late."

She hung around until it was time for dinner. Before leaving she flashed me a telling look, reminding me that I had to tell someone about Reese.

I don't know. I have to think that over. Right now I need some peace and quiet. My head hurts from the Qualihydrone, and I barely feel like eating. The steaming stew they've given me smells so good though. Hmm . . . I think I'll try a spoonful.

December 21, 2602: 0030 hours

Big mistake trying that stew. I couldn't stop at a spoonful, finished it all up. And now I'm paying for being so greedy. My stomach has been churning non-stop and I wish I could walk around. But this hopeless tube!

Wait . . . what's that noise . . . the nurse is not supposed to come back in another hour.

December 21, 2602: 0100 hours

Guess who was here to see me? Reese Michael Jarvis Worthington the Fifth. He snuck into the quarantine floor, past the guards and the monitors, and found me.

He smiled on seeing me, seeming relieved that I was still awake.

He knew my name also. "Hey, Dee Dee," he said.

"You're Reese," I replied.

"I came to say I'm sorry. First of all, you didn't get infected by the real Roban-Qu. It was just a fake—an imitation. The imitation was not meant for you either. It got transferred by accident."

"*Was* you then?"

He nodded, very reluctantly.

"Have you told anyone about me?" he asked next.

"About you? Umm . . ."

"You must've told your friend, right?"

He guessed about Pompy. "It's only Pompy," I tried to explain. Then decided to push him a bit. "But what were you planning to do with the imitation? Where did you get it from anyway?"

"I cook my imitations." He sounded so casual, as if brewing non-toxic strains of the most dangerous virus ever known was commonplace and . . . easy.

"You *what*? Why?"

"Because they're expensive to buy, so I make my own. And the quality is much better anyway."

"No. No, no," I fumbled. It was a strange conversation with the strangest kid I've ever come across. "I mean . . . why do you need imitations at all?"

"Because the real virus would be toxic. People could be killed, and I don't want that."

"Ugh. Didn't mean that either. I—"

"Just for fun."

"Fun?"

He shrugged. "Imagine what Sapoor would do if he found the mark on his arm."

"It was for Sapoor? Why?"

"He's on my hit list, that's why."

"Hit list? What are you? An assassin?"

His green eyes flashed for a second, but then they drooped.

"I was in Hall 2 with my friend Kas and Sapoor wouldn't let me stay there. He doesn't like Kas. He thinks Kas is mentally unsound. And Dad thought his advice was good, so he had me moved."

"Where are you now?"

"In 6. I don't know anyone there."

"I'm in 6 too."

"I know."

"*We* could be friends," I said.

His face brightened. "You're not angry with me?"

"Why should I be? It was just an accident."

"Your friend Pompy won't be thrilled."

"That's my problem."

For a second all was quiet, and then something crashed outside and someone whimpered.

Reese sprang to his feet. "I have to leave. The guard I had hypnotized must have woken up."

"What? Hypnotized? How? And how will you get past him now?"

"That's my problem," he replied, and slipped past the doorway.

I don't know if I did the right thing offering to be his friend. Pompy is going to be mad at me for sure. But the boy is interesting. I mean, who goes around cooking up fake virus soup? No one on this boring, humongous spaceship has any sense of fun. We've been drifting in space for a whole year and we will keep on going for days, weeks, months, in search of a possibility called Plebius. We're not even sure we'll reach it. I'm tired of serious faces and of worrying about our doom. I'd rather have a little fun.

December 21, 2602: 1700 hours

I'm free! I'm out of that crazy quarantine tube and back in my room.

Pompy isn't speaking with me. I told her about Reese. She told me that falling for a bad boy was "clichéd" and "galling." Said she didn't want anything to do with such "stereotypical idiocy." I had no idea that I was falling for anyone until she told me, thought I simply liked the excitement Reese brought with him.

Pompy says we won't last long. That Reese just needs a loyal sidekick, like any other show-folk. And she would have nothing to do with brainless lackeys.

Well, whatever!

<u>December 24, 2602: 1800 hours</u>

That boy, Reese, sure has a thing against Sapoor. He can't stop blaming Sapoor for separating him from his friend Kas. All he thinks about is a chance to get back at the principal master. He has come up with another outrageous plan.

Today Sapoor announced a tour of our lab on Thursday. Reese walked up to me right after class was over. Staring at me with his dead-quiet eyes, he asked, "Did you get that?"

"What?"

"Sapoor's visiting us on experiment day."

"So?"

"Time to make him pay."

I'm not sure how I agreed to assist him. Guess he's too new a friend to fall out with, and his plan sounds fail-proof. And every time I think of a rainbow-colored principal master as a final prize, I can't stop the giggles.

We're going to sneak out of the hall after midnight, Reese and I. We have to prep the equipment. Reese thinks that Rushi, our class monitor, will be the one to demonstrate the distillation experiment. I agree. So, the plan is to paint the inside of her flask with the stainer pigments and make tiny perforations on the front of her collecting chamber. These tiny holes will be enough to stress the chamber once it is full and it will rip along the stress lines.

I'm a tiny bit worried. What if something explodes and hurts someone? Reese has assured me that's not gonna happen.

"I've done this many times, Dee Dee," he said. "Nothing's going to explode. It's just a harmless prank, that's all."

Fingers crossed.

December 26, 2602: 1300 hours

Sapoor has put me in solitary isolation.

It's the worst possible disciplinary action, ever. The room is cozy and even stocked with paper books. But I'm alone. And I'll be kept here for three days. Alone. With nothing but books. This punishment must've been designed by a madman.

Know what got me here? Reese's prank of course.

Reese was right. Nothing exploded. Nothing hurt anyone either. At least not physically. I mean, if you disregard stained faces, that is. Rushi started bawling on seeing the colors on her face once the cloud of stain-vapors cleared. I think she overreacted. It's not like her face was stained forever. It will only be there for a few days, maybe a week at most.

But Rushi took it hard. Reese and I couldn't tell her that we hadn't expected Sapoor to walk over to Jun's table midway through the experiment, or that there was no stopping it at that point other than wishing and praying that the holes we made into Rushi's collection chamber wouldn't make it rip. But, rip it did. Within seconds, the chamber released all its contents onto Rushi's shocked face.

I've noticed that once things start falling apart, they fall apart pretty fast and take even dependable things down with them. Pompy, for instance. Somehow, she had a hunch that Reese was involved in this, and somehow she managed to direct the teachers to his storage. The evidence they found was . . . damaging. Reese was taken away to solitary right away. It didn't end there — I was called into questioning next. Pompy smirked at me as I was walking into the principal master's chamber, the same Pompy who was my best friend up until a few days ago. Later, I found out that she gave Sapoor my journal as evidence. I was so sad and angry at the same time that I practically screamed my everlasting allegiance to Reese. Held my head high when they sent me away to this room.

I'm never, ever going to speak to Pompy ever again.

<u>December 29, 2602: 1300 hours</u>

I met Evie today. Right after our solitary was over. She was waiting at the gate of Hall 6 for us. Evie, she told us, is short for Evelyn. Evie had thick glasses on, her greasy, uncombed hair seemed hurriedly tied into braids, and her pant legs ended an inch above her ankles.

"I'm the new Warden of Hall #6," she declared, hugging each of us. "I'm here to escort you home. I have some nice warm soup waiting for you too."

Didn't that sound sweet? I thought it did. But Reese made a face.

Pompy was lying in her bunk, reading, when I got to my room. The way she hid her face behind that reader, it seemed like she was trying to hide a smile. The whole of me wanted to scream at the girl, but I didn't. Instead I went about my business and Pompy peeked every now and then to watch. A few minutes later, she bolted upright in her bed. Guess she couldn't take my silence anymore.

"I didn't mean to tell them about you, you know," she blurted. "I only wanted them to know about *him*. And I don't want you to get mixed up with that boy."

I didn't reply.

"Rushi's face is still a mess. And Warden Morales got reassigned. All because of *him*."

"How's that? Why did the warden—"

"Sapoor didn't appreciate that you two snuck out of the hall at night, so he brought Warden Evelyn, Evie, to replace him."

"Hmm . . ."

"Evie's supposed keep an extra eye on you. You should be careful, Dee. What if they blacklist you? You're thirteen. You're past the age of getting charged with just a delinquent card. Do you want to be thrown out of Decima? Reese's dad is the sec-comm, so he can get away with these things. You can't."

I told her I'd think about staying away from Reese. I lied of course.

But Pompy has got me thinking. She does have a point. Reese can, what Gramps would say, pull strings. I, on the other hand, have no such string to pull. I *am* the string for my family. But Reese is my friend, and Pompy, by reporting me to Sapoor, can be a friend no more.

January 9, 2603: 1900 hours

Reese has gone hyper-crazy nuts. He keeps planning and plotting.

He doesn't tell me all of his plans though. A few I know about before they happen, but most I don't. It's because I keep this journal. And it got us caught one time already.

"Can't keep writing confessions in there, Dee Dee," he told me the other day, scowling. "You'll get us in trouble."

I didn't argue with him, but I knew I wouldn't stop writing. I promised Gramps I would keep an honest journal, and I'm not going to give that up for anyone or anything. I only have to find a better and safer place to store it.

Anyway, today I woke up to doors slamming, the sound of running feet, and Evie yelling above all the din. Took me a while to figure what happened; the doors of all the hall bathrooms had gone missing. Overnight. Vanished, just like that. If someone has not been in a situation like this, they will never know what such a thing means. Was a genuine emergency, life or death type of thing. A hundred kids waking up in a world where all the bathrooms are as good as gone. It's a living nightmare!

Sapoor came by, repairers as well. Most of us had been temporarily relocated to an adjacent hall by then. Sapoor was furious, and Evie was clueless. They questioned Reese for hours, but found not a shred of evidence that could connect him to the door abductions.

"You worry for no reason," Reese assured me later.

"Was it you?" I had to ask.

"What are you talking about?"

Flashed him a telling look. "The doors."

"You think I could remove twenty-five doors?" Reese chuckled, as if I had asked the weirdest question in the world. "What am I, Superman?"

I've been thinking about his reply a lot. Reese is right; this couldn't be his doing. There had to be an army of Reeses to pull this off.

<u>March 19, 2603: 1900 hours</u>

Sapoor is sending us all to solitary isolation. Yes, all of us. The entire Hall 6. We will have to take turns because the isolation floor cannot hold more than twenty at a time.

Why? Because someone set up a viewing stream of Sapoor at a gambling table. Gambling isn't illegal, but it shows you in poor light, particularly if you're the principal master at Decima. Sort of reflects badly on Decima too.

I heard Sapoor's bosses called him to a discussion. Some good it did—he came back from that meeting and set us up with the solitary.

It'll take a while for Sapoor to calm down. Truth is, Hall 6 has become the most notorious hall on Seeder 5. Things just keep happening; if one day a dozen hairy spiders are set loose in the study room, the next day the warden's food is spiked with Aceio pepper. And now this!

I doubt that Reese is the mastermind behind all of these pranks. It seems to me like a whole group of anonymous pranksters have taken up the fight against Sapoor. Doubt if they even know of Reese's cause or they have simply dived into the mayhem just because it's fun.

Each time something out of the ordinary happens, Evie, Sapoor's right hand in Hall 6, calls Reese to interrogation. I think it's unfair to single Reese out, but Evie doesn't seem to care much for fairness. She gets a slightest confirmation of her suspicions and off Reese goes to solitary.

Evie has been making Reese miserable in other ways too. She allots him extra tasks around the hall, she has increased his study sessions, and she has cut his free hours in half. Obviously, Sapoor is the brains behind the evil operation, and Evie is his facilitator.

<u>May 05, 2603: 2100 hours</u>

Today's another day that'll stick in my mind forever.

Right after supper hours, Reese rushed up to me. "Got something. Come on, Dee Dee."

When we finally found an isolated corner to talk, he said, "I have something on Evie. We're going to use that get her off my case. I'm tired of her bothering me."

"Please don't—"

He cut me off right away.

"Dee Dee, forget about it. You don't have to do this."

"No. I want to help. But, please be careful."

"I'm always careful."

"What've you got?"

"Papers. Evie forged her papers. She stole an identity."

"What?"

No one in their right mind forges papers or steals identities, and certainly not someone on a Seeder. Forgery of identification papers is a criminal act punishable by death, has been so since before the Flood. If found guilty, Evie could be sent to the galleys at the bottommost level of the spaceship. Would probably be dead within days.

"Evie forged her papers," Reese repeated calmly.

"How do you know?"

"I know. I have my sources. And proof."

"Who knows about this?"

"Just you and I . . . for now."

"What will you do with it?"

"Start by telling Sapoor and then Dad."

He was going to bring her down.

We marched into Evie's room, a defiant and joyful Reese leading the way. I rushed to keep up.

"I'm going to report this," Reese declared after he made his charge. Evie simply stared, her face pale and her eyes seeming even bigger behind those thick glasses.

"P-please don't," she stuttered to life after a very long pause. One thing was clear from the way she reacted: whatever Reese had accused her of was indeed true. "I didn't have a choice."

"You tell Sapoor that."

How Sapoor showed up in Evie's room so quickly I'll never figure out. It was as if he was expecting to get that call from Reese all along.

"You don't want to do this," the principal master said after he heard everything. Felt odd. Then I realized . . . *he knew*.

"You knew." Reese came to the same conclusion.

"Yes."

Reese let out a loud chuckle. He sounded delighted. "That's good. Now I'll report you too, and be done with you both."

"Reese, I don't think you should," Sapoor said.

"Really? And why not?"

"Because if you do, you'll hurt your friend."

"My friend? Kas?"

Sapoor nodded.

"Explain," Reese demanded.

Sapoor fidgeted a little. Looked around the room for a minute. Then slumping into a chair, he scratched his head for a while. After that, he started.

"Kas, as you know, was one of the finest ones drafted into the Surrogate Project. His algorithms helped us pinpoint the Earth Surrogates. He had to be a part of one of the Seeders, which he is. But, as you know, he is also a carrier of the — "

"Roban-Qu. I know."

"Roban-Qu?" I practically screamed. There was a person on this Seeder infected with the Roban-Qu? And these people were talking like that was a normal thing?

"Yes, but he's a super-elite controller, meaning he can somehow suppress the virus to less than five copies per milliliter of his blood for decades. Compare that to a full-blown diseased person who will have a million copies of the virus per milliliter within a day of being infected."

"You mean the disease doesn't progress inside of him," I inferred, or tried to.

"You're right. But, Reese, your father didn't want you to be around him given there was a chance — "

"Dad?"

Sapoor sighed. "The sec-commander wanted you removed."

Don't know how Reese took that, he was looking away from all of us. But he sure took a long time to speak again.

"All right. What's that got to do with Ms. Evelyn?"

Sapoor threw a questioning glance at Evie, who replied with a morose nod.

"Kas contracted the disease when he was a baby along with his family. His family — his father, three siblings — died within a week, except for Kas and his mother. She had a genetic marker that made her resistant to the bug."

"And?"

"Kas was given a spot on the Seeder without much reservation. We needed him, his brain. But his mother was not deemed a necessity. She was expendable and even a risk given that she had contracted the Roban-Qu once."

Sort of had a hunch at this point. Reese must have as well, because those dead-quiet eyes of his started scanning Sapoor's face and Evie's too.

"I had known Kas since he was five. He had given up his childhood to the Surrogate Project and now he was denied the only thing he wanted, the only family he had left—his mother. So I—"

"Forged papers for her?"

"I did."

Felt a little dizzy right about then. I didn't even want to look at Evie. I fell back a couple of steps away from the woman.

"You've had it also?"

Evie looked embarrassed. "Don't worry. I'm clean. I test myself every day to be sure. I wouldn't risk anyone, especially children."

No matter what she said, it was scary. Standing three feet away from a person who had once carried the Roban-Qu was not a thrilling experience. Realized quickly how stupid I was. Evie said she was clean now, and I still couldn't get past the fact that she had once been infected. She suffered through the infection and won the battle against the Roban-Qu—*that* was the important part. And I was not willing to consider the facts out of my stupid fear, just like everyone else.

"So, Reese," Sapoor continued, "now that you've heard everything, you decide."

"You know what? You put me and Kas back together and I'll forget all about this."

Sapoor blinked, clearly not believing a word.

"But the sec-commander doesn't want you near him. He won't approve this—"

"You have to figure that out."

Sapoor stayed quiet for a second. Then his questioning gaze turned to me.

Reese chuckled. "Oh yes, Dee Dee. She can keep secrets. Won't you?"

I nodded. This secret? I would happily carry it to my grave.

Reese nudged me out of the room. "Go on, Dee Dee, I'll see you tomorrow."

Stayed behind himself. Guess he had to discuss his relocation plans with Sapoor and Evie.

That was an hour ago. I've been waiting for Reese to knock on my door to tell me what happened after I left. But something tells me that I won't see him again. By tomorrow morning, Reese will have vanished, once again, just like that.

GIMP

The Frecais Gate Incident was a game changer in more ways than one. It ended lives and made new ones possible. It made heroes out of regular people and martyrs out of scoundrels. It changed destinies, and although we didn't know it then, it started changing our collective future.

A lot of people were touched by the incident. Take me for instance. Before that, I was an enviable specimen of a human. After being captured and having my foot ripped apart, I can only hobble. Maybe you can guess that's where my name comes from, Gimp, kindly bestowed on me by Chief Engineer Nassur. I hold no grudge against the Suckers. Crippled or not, at least they let me live. If it were me and the HS, no traitors would have lived to see another day.

They caught me at the switching station disconnecting power from the electrified inner fences at the Frecais Gate. I feigned innocence, told them it was a mistake. But the fact that thousands of my comrades picked the exact moment and that exact section of the fence I disabled to break in gave me away. One guard shot my right foot with his laser blaster. The last thing I remember was my blood flying all over the station, painting it red from floor to ceiling, and the pale, jagged edges of my bones sticking out of the mangled flesh.

Sometime later, I woke up in a tiny cell to two men inspecting my feet.

"He'll live," one man said. "The right leg is as good as gone, but he'll live."

"I'll take him. He'll make the perfect help."

"Are you sure, Chief Engineer? He's a generic spy. You know of the Frecais G—"

"What do I look like? Stupid?"

"No . . . but . . ."

"Fix him up. I'll get him released into my custody."

"All right."

In all honesty, I simply got lucky that Chief Engineer Nassur happened by the cell where I was being held and realized I could be useful. How else can I make sense of my being alive, on the Seeder no less, after having infiltrated their system and aiding in the Frecais Gate showdown? My comrades were killed in droves, but we got a lot of the Suckers also — hurt them enough to make them want to destroy my leg.

***

Chief Engineer Nassur was prone to fits of anger. He also gave his soul to an everlasting spell of suspicion.

Thanks to that, his wife left him, taking with her their two children, twin daughters, who still come by to visit their father once in a while. This was back when he was on Earth, an event that traumatized him and drove him more to the edge. The man adored his daughters, and the strange thing was that he never lost his temper with the twins, and he was someone who would fly off the handle at the slightest provocation. Once the girls spilled lemonade all over the blueprint of a new transformer he was working on and ruined it. I feared for their lives, but Nassur didn't even flinch.

The GG tolerated his temper because he was a genius. The engines on the Seeders were designed by him, as was the framework of the electrical system. Without him, the Surrogate Project would have stayed a work in progress forever. But, Nassur's brilliance made the GG's dreams come true. So, while not a poster child of the Project, Nassur remained the eccentric virtuoso you were obligated to tolerate and even pamper for the greater benefit.

That was also why Nassur was able to extract me from the holding cell and appoint me his personal assistant, butler, manservant, without anyone visibly raising a brow. For me, it was a stroke of luck. I accepted the chance, thinking that maybe a spectacular destiny of some sort awaited me.

I tolerated his temper the same way a dog puts up with its abusive master's kicks. It doesn't have a choice, or it doesn't care enough to find if there is a choice. The truth about me was that even a thousand kicks didn't negate the gift of second life Nassur granted me. He got me out for his self-serving reasons, I was well aware, but still, I stayed grateful.

His suspicion, while less evident from the outside, ate away at the man from the inside. He was mistrustful of everything — of his peers stealing his inventions, of his subordinates plotting to undermine him, of random people poisoning his food. He trusted no one, except me perhaps. I suppose he figured that since I was a documented prisoner alive solely at his discretion, I wouldn't dare hurt him. Also, he needed a spy to keep an eye on everyone else around him. And he didn't know of any other than me. Whatever his reasons, they were why I was spared of being hooked to death over the Frecais Gate.

Nassur was a nuisance of an employer. Lately, however, the chief engineer had grown unusually volatile. There were more flung dishes, more elaborate cursing, and . . . conversation. He talked to me more over the last week than he had in three years.

"I won't let them crucify me," he declared one day while eating his breakfast. "I only have to keep them on a tight leash."

Placing the medley of fruits, warmed up just a notch like he demanded, I started tasting a sampling of the fare. The man wouldn't take a bite before I tasted his food for him — so much for trust. A chunk of sour pineapple was torturing my taste buds, but I still nodded dutifully.

"Are you listening, Gimp?" he shouted, slamming his fists on the table.

I hastened to reply. "Sir, yes. Of course."

"Chimera is set to begin," he said in a feverish tone. "I have my population list all the way down to the second- and third-tier leaders."

"Chimera, sir?"

"You don't know about Chimera? Aren't you supposed to be a spy?" he yelled. "Can't believe I've been wasting my rations on a mutt like you."

I heard of Chimera — a highly classified program that would affect the entire population on the Seeder. Other than that, Chimera was not discussed much; people got really touchy when that word was spoken. Not that I wanted to know more, I preferred to make do with whatever little was needed to keep my remaining limbs intact.

I told Nassur what I knew and he calmed down some.

"Once we reach Plebius, the Morpheus population will be divided up," he explained in a thoughtful voice. "There'll probably be twenty sub-populations — Chimeras 1 to 20. Each will be assigned an area on Plebius to build their community and survive — a final pass-through of the survival-of-the-fittest argument."

"Every settlement for itself then," I said, thinking how fierce the battle was going to be with what were given — a planet that had barely been charted, tools that hadn't been proven, and people who even after being three years on this ship together, scarcely knew or cared about each other.

My words didn't help him. Baring his tobacco-stained yellow teeth, he hissed instead.

"Yes, Gimp. I know. I need to build the best community of them all, do you understand?"

I didn't quite get it. What was stopping him from doing that?

"You can, sir."

"Really? Says you, the crippled captured spy?"

The best way to handle his insults was to let them pass — that I had learned. It worked again. Nassur breathed rapidly a few times in an effort to collect himself.

"Would've been better if I wasn't given a community," he said finally. "They could've given me a place in someone else's and I'd be happy. But no."

I knew something that Nassur probably didn't want to be reminded of—no one wanted Nassur on their team. Once, the man badgered a brand-new flux drive with a pipe until it looked like pancake crumbles because it failed to keep its pace. Another time, he almost choked an intern to death, because the kid didn't get an equation right. Genius or not—everyone had to draw a line somewhere with Nassur.

"No one likes me," the chief engineer rambled on. "Everyone will be plotting to bring me down. I'll fail. That's what that dank Perrogi wants. Then he'll have me eliminated and sent off for good."

Perrogi was the commander of the Seeder. He had no love lost for Nassur. Rumors said Perrogi had even started a campaign to move Nassur to Seeder 2 that took off from Territory 103. But his second-in-command Worthington wanted to have a genius like Nassur around. Maybe the sec-commander figured Nassur could help in case something went wrong during the long journey to Plebius.

"Can't have traitors among my crew, Gimp," he said, letting out a resigned sigh. "I can't be looking over my shoulder all the time. Can't let them sabotage me."

If only the man could let go of his suspicions and trust people a little. He wouldn't, I knew very well. I had to think of something else. I needed something to keep Nassur from falling apart, at least until we reached Plebius.

"We could come up with a plan, sir," I tried to reassure the man. "We can try to figure out who's with you and who's not. That way you can put the people you can trust in the right places."

He looked at me with hopeful eyes. But the hope drained quickly and all that was left was ridicule.

"How do you plan to do that, genius?"

To be honest, I didn't quite know. Nassur was correct—no one liked him. No one who was worth anything would want to be in his community—that was also true. But we had to figure this out. I thought improving the chief engineer's image could be a good starting point.

"Maybe we can arrange a feast for the second- and third-tier leaders?"

"And hand out candies?" he scoffed, and dug into his eggs.

"No, sir," I continued fearlessly. "We can talk to them and try to sense who you could trust."

"Like that'll work."

"It's better than not doing anything."

He stared at me and kept on staring. My muscles tensed; his being so still was unusual. When would he snap? What if he threw that knife at me?

"All right." He nodded after breathless eons trickled past. "Why are you still standing here then? Go plan that party."

When I was at the kitchen door, he yelled, "Gimp, remember, I better not fail."

As if that was news to me. The man didn't like to lose. Not even in matters he was not good at.

***

The bunch near the sweet end of the service line caught my eye fairly quickly. I could tell they were Nassur's nemesis — young upstarts, perfect assets for any community but Nassur's. The way their eyes roamed, darting from face to face, innocent yet hungry in their need for success, it could only mean one thing: they had an agenda.

Picking up a service tray stacked with an eye-catching array of cakes, I started in their direction. The girl in green and gold stood in the center. Her frosted glass-like eyes stood out on her smoky complexion, but the most remarkable feature on her lean frame was the fiery hair. She was a science officer, a well-ranked one as well, I deduced, counting the stripes on her cuffs. She kept good company too. Both men flanking her were commandants — their all-black uniforms with silver-starred shoulder straps announced that loudly. I tried to read the nametags on their chests, elegant little things I had put together a few nights ago to help people get to know each other easily. Now, my hard work would come to some real use.

"Sir?" I swiveled the tray in front of the trio with the flourish of a peacock unfurling its plume.

The man to the right of the science officer fell back a step in an instant, like deer that smelled a predator. His eyes looked like ice, his mouth rigid. His face melted into a lopsided, impish smile the next moment, like the sun breaking through the rainclouds in the blink of an eye. No one but a trained operative like me would have caught the shift. This man, I made a mental note, must have been part of covert-ops of some sort. I also noted his name: Scott, L.

"No, thank you," he said in a melodious drawl that could only have been fostered in the northern territories. He jabbed his thumb playfully in the direction of the other man in the group. "Commandant Hung, over there, can help lighten your load, I'm pretty sure."

Commandant Hung rolled his eyes and shook his head as the red-haired woman burst out laughing.

"Lars isn't wrong, is he, Iseul?" she said.

"When is he ever wrong?"

They seemed like nice kids, in their mid-twenties, blessed overachievers who must have waltzed their way to the Seeders.

"Hey, server, you." The call made me turn away from the trio, but not before Commandant Hung helped himself to a pair of servings off my tray. Commandant Scott was right after all, I thought, restraining a grin as I hobbled, tray in hand, toward a pleasantly smiling Nassur.

"You idiot," Nassur snarled when I reached him. I knew that tone; he was mad enough to hurl things. I learned over the years to keep my head down when he was in one of his moods, so I busied myself counting the spots on the fake marble flooring. "Didn't I tell you to figure out people?"

I was doing just that. Why didn't he get it?

"And you're wasting time talking to those third-tier kids. You should talk to the second-tier engineers over there." He nodded in the direction of the podium where a few of Nassur's current peers stood in a tight huddle.

"I think the kids—" I started, forgetting my place for a second.

"Do you want to lose your other leg as well?" Nassur hissed, his glare burning my face. "I will have it ripped off if you don't get me some intel by tonight, you understand?"

"Yes, sir."

"Don't stand there and 'sir' me." The words barely made it through his gnashed teeth. Loudly enough for others to hear, he added, "Move it, Gimp."

I missed having both my legs working. Nassur's words ringing in my ears, my back burning with his murderous glare, sneaky glances people shot at me—I couldn't get away quickly enough. I wondered how much more of this humiliation I would have to endure. And if there would be any escape in this lifetime.

She accosted me as I headed toward the podium.

"Sorry to stop you, Mr. Server," the frosty-eyed science officer with fiery hair said with an apologetic smile. "I was so busy making fun of Iseul that I forgot to pick a plate for myself."

"Yes, of course, please." I offered the tray. "That one with the bitter-chocolate ganache is the one to die for, I was told."

She smiled. "Everything all right with the chief engineer back there?" she said casually, her gaze flicking questioningly at my face as her slender fingers wrapped around the pastry I suggested.

"Of course. Why would you think—"

"We have ears, man." I had not noticed that Commandant Hung approached. His hand swooped in and captured a white froth-topped confection. "Eyes too. And we know that guy's history. So . . ."

He paused to tackle the frothy top of the cake.

"If there's any trouble that man's causing you," he muttered, biting busily into the remaining piece, "you need to reach out to someone."

For a few moments I stopped breathing. These were, indeed, the people Nassur had been dreading. Perceptive, charismatic and everything Nassur was not. I read the signs right, and Nassur was wrong. His challenge wouldn't come from his equals, but from somewhere he was not expecting.

"I think there's a misunderstanding." I knew the chief engineer, and I was not about to get these kids in trouble. There was no need for war. At least not at the moment. "All is perfectly well and—"

"I don't think so," the girl cut my assurances off. "You see, I know *your* history as well. Had it been up to me, you'd not be on this Seeder. Yet, you are. And since you are, you're equal to anyone else and should be treated as such. You're not someone's property. If they let you free, you should live free without fear."

It was quickly getting uncomfortable . . . and unsafe. Simply standing there listening to them was not prudent. So, I looked around for the missing third member of their team, Commandant Scott. He was an arm's distance away, talking feverishly over his stream-comm, his face darker than before.

"Kat's right." Hung's hand grabbed one more offering from my tray. "You could get Nassur written off if you wanted to. That name he calls you has no place on a Seeder. It goes against the GG's Codes of Justice. This is a fresh start for humanity, remember?"

"You can come to us anytime," the girl insisted. "You shouldn't think there's no one to stand up for you."

She didn't realize that help didn't matter. Not anymore. I didn't have a fight-worthy cause—lost it the moment I left Earth on this Seeder. Now, there was only breathing in and breathing out.

"Hey, Kat, come listen to this." The urgency in Commandant Scott's voice was obvious. Science Officer Katryn stopped nibbling at the edge of her chocolate-ganache and stepped away toward him in haste. Commandant Hung picked up another cake from the tray before following suit.

Breathing a sigh of relief, I hobbled toward what had been my destination before Science Officer Katryn ambushed me. I was in desperate need of some intel for my keeper. The trio I left behind whispered agitatedly. I caught the whiff on one sentence: "It's official. Chimera has begun. This is it, our sub-population."

***

Chief Engineer Nassur's party fizzled out quickly that night. I wondered if "Chimera" announcement had something to do with it. Right after my favorite trio huddled together, everyone else seemed eager to leave; I suppose no one was thrilled to find out they were put in Nassur's camp. In a way, it was a good thing. I had more time to wrap things up.

Supervision of the catering staff was not as easy as it sounded — tallying accounts, disbursing funds, and working out the net reserves kept me up until the early hours of the morning. Nassur would demand an update when he awoke, and since I had little of the "intel" he demanded, I had to make sure I had other means to please him. At least, I needed enough to keep him from hacking my good leg off. I didn't hear them come in.

"Still burning oil?" Wylan's voice was slick like always. He was one of the scoundrels who made good use of the Frecais Gate Incident. Wylan Ross, a former foot soldier of HS, was now a self-proclaimed messiah of the downtrodden on Seeder 5.

"Your loyalty to Nassur is unbelievable." She was there as well, influencer, puppeteer, spinner of webs — Avril Red. "Did he call you names at tonight's feast? How dare he? You should report his actions."

Wylan pulled up a tall stool and installed himself on it. "I've always told you so," he said, fondly caressing his goatee.

He never said such a thing to me, and he knew it. He had not budged an inch to get me out of the mess I was in on the day of the Frecais Gate Incident. He was not one to risk blowing his own cover for anyone else. Even later, when Nassur got me out, Wylan only came by to say that I should do anything it took to survive, that HS still had plans I could help with, that I had to stay put. Those days passed in a haze and the Seeder had already taken off when I came to realize the trick these scoundrels had pulled. They volunteered to get embedded in the Population not because they wanted to fight for the cause, but because it was the best chance they had to escape Earth.

Per Hell's Spawn directives, every operative was supposed to stop the Seeder from leaving or die trying. But these people had their own plans. The realization upset me at first, then I thought of myself—I was no different. I, too, did everything I could do so I could live. I didn't try enough to stop the Seeder. If I did, maybe . . .

"Wylie, aren't you glad that he didn't listen to you?" Avril Red flicked her shiny mane and tapped Wylan's shoulder sharply. "Now, we have the right man in the right spot."

I put on my vacant face, but deep in the pit of my stomach, tiny muscles clenched. This had to be something novel, a plot from a new angle, like everything was with Avril Red. There was a reason I avoided this duo; they were frauds who respected nothing.

"We need your help," Wylan gulped. He still feared me, I noted with pleasure. "You might've noticed that this Seeder is once again divided. Even among the elites, there are those who are not pure-gened enough. People are kept separated by the floors, every class is fed different and treated different. Red and I, we keep fighting for the less fortunate. In a way, we're still fighting for the cause we fought for so long on Earth. Once we reach Plebius, we will build our army once again."

Fighting for the cause. I wished away a wry chuckle inside me. They didn't know a thing about the cause. Right after the Frecais Gate, Wylan started circulating tales of his family, including that of his two-year-old child, being victims of the massacre. The fib reached me much later, but it did nonetheless. His tragic tale, spun the right way by Red, earned him a spotlight of sympathy. Wylan became the martyr who had lost everything — a champion of all those who had lost, of those who found the Seeder divided along the same lines of prejudice they thought they had left behind on Earth. Only I knew the truth.

Red leaned forward, her luminous eyes holding my gaze. "You'll be in Nassur's Chimera, of course. So, we could benefit much if you could feel out the population there. You've always been so good at figuring out people."

She was right, I was good. That's why I was the first HS operative to be sent undercover. It was a long time ago, so long in fact that I could barely recall life before I got into the bunkers. It was the nineties of the last century, the beginning of us, the generics in Sucker-say, starting to figure out the truth behind the conspiracy theories. My call came in 2989. At Hell's Spawn, we were always ready, we had to be. I was too. Never had a family, so there was no one to say good-bye to, except Leela. I would've married that girl if I had stayed out. I still dream about her sometimes, but nowadays she hovers like an untouchable specter and never shows her face — maybe because I don't remember it anymore.

"There's bound to be some anger in his Chimera," Wylan jumped in, suddenly emboldened by Red. "We could feed on that weakness. Will you help?"

Wylan did not have parents or even a girl of his own. That child who perished at the Frecais Gate was not his, that I was pretty certain. And he knew that I knew. Heck, I knew more than that — I knew the covers of every HS operative on this Seeder. I knew everything from their names to everything else that had been planted on their bios. I created those bios myself back when I was zooming up the ranks of HS. Another year outside and I would've led Hell's Spawn. But then my call got me underground.

"Of course he will, Wylie," Red said. "He can't ignore the cause and all the sacrifices we've made all these years."

I had to smile. One right move was all they needed, and they had just about picked the right one. Everyone on this Seeder knew my story; I would be the perfect person to convert half-willing hearts. And true, Nassur's unit was probably full of dissenters already. However, the best part for them wanting me on their side was something else—choosing them would mean every secret I knew about HS and its stowaway operatives would stay secrets forever.

A vague smile and a vaguer nod was all they needed, and the duo slithered out soon after, leaving me alone with my thoughts.

***

Tonight is a night of new beginnings. After completing Nassur's tallies of the party, I don't spread my palm under the med-vender next to my bed. For the first time since they crippled me, I refuse to use the tiny green pill that would transport my mind into few a dark hours of oblivion. Instead, I pull out a paper and make a list. First comes the queen and then comes the rest, faceless pieces in my game of chess. Only I know who those pieces really are—they are people I can use, people I need to swing, people I have to eliminate. This will be a good war. Even though it could be my last one, it would have to be the one I will win.

It has been a bountiful day.

***

CHIMERA IS COMING...

ABOUT THE AUTHOR

Shatarupa G. Basu is an engineer by training, but she likes to call herself a dreamer. Her world is filled with wondrous machines, cybernetic robots, dragons and sorcerers, some of which escape into the pages of her books.

She enjoys traveling to faraway places. Her writing is often inspired by the people she meets in these beautiful lands. Her stories are a celebration of the influences from her travels around the world.

Ms. Basu is also an avid nature photographer. When she is not busy writing, she enjoys gardening, music, and spending time outdoors with her family.

Ms. Basu resides in Maryland with her husband and daughter.

Find out about more about the author and her works at sgbasu.com.

www.ingramcontent.com/pod-product-compliance
Lightning Source LLC
Chambersburg PA
CBHW020631130626
46552CB00003B/1179